THE IMPRISONED
SPLENDOR

By the same author

Vadiraja's Refutation of Sankara's Non-Dualism
The Rich Man
Sing Like the Whippoorwill
Sunlit Waters
Thomas
The Afterlife Unveiled

THE IMPRISONED SPLENDOR

A novel by

STAFFORD BETTY

www.whitecrowbooks.com

Acknowledgements

S PECIAL thanks to my former student Kathleen O'Neal Gear, co-author of the celebrated "People" novels, for her critically important suggestion that I rearrange the order of the chapters and begin with the crash; to my spiritual soul brother Michael Tymn for introducing me to Jon Beecher, the only publisher on the planet who could appreciate what I am trying to do here; to Jon himself, publisher of White Crow Books, whose expert vetting turned many an awkward or stiff passage into friendlier, clearer prose; and to my wife, Monica, for being patient with me when I sometimes put my craft ahead of everything else.

Dedicated to my mother,
Lillian Conover Betty,
who died earlier this year
anticipating the great journey ahead.

"Truth is within ourselves; it takes no rise
From outward things, whate'er you may believe.
There is an inmost centre in us all,
Where truth abides in fulness; and around,
Wall upon wall, the gross flesh hems it in,
This perfect, clear perception - which is truth.
A baffling and perverting carnal mesh
Binds it, and makes all error: and to KNOW
Rather consists in opening out a way
Whence the imprisoned splendour may escape,
Than in effecting entry for a light
Supposed to be without." — Robert Browning

"Life's splendor forever lies in wait about each one of us in all its fullness,
but veiled from view, deep down, invisible, far off." — Franz Kafka

"Death is not extinguishing the light; it is putting out the lamp because
dawn has come." — Rabindranath Tagore

To the Reader

THE action in this novel takes place mostly in the world beyond death. It did not grow out of my unaided imagination, but out of years of careful paranormal research. Writers of historical fiction meticulously study the setting of their story before they begin their work. It was the same with me, except that the cultures and geographies I studied don't belong to our world. They are at least as fascinating as ours and make a superlative backdrop for a novel, as you are about to discover.

Contents

Chapter 1

K IRAN Kulkarni found himself in the first row, aisle seat, of an Indian Airlines plane headed for Bombay out of Madras. Tapping on his forehead with his pen and looking up into space, he mulled over an argument for a paper he would present at a philosophy conference in Philadelphia. Suddenly he squirmed in his seat and dug out his wallet. There they were, his children: golden-faced Ravi, dignified and almost too serious for his thirteen years; and blue-eyed little Sonya with her curly light brown hair, his little angel of eight who looked like her mother. God how he missed them! Only four more days till he was back home in California.

In the seat to his left a coffee-colored man leaned his head against the window and half-blocked the sinking sun as it hung over the gray cloudscape below. The monsoons were on, not a break anywhere in the clouds. Kiran wondered if it would be raining in Bombay. He closed his eyes . . .

Kanchipuram. His mind drifted off to the raggedy palm-reader plying her trade under a large margosa tree. He had the habit of worrying about the world's destitute – about the only virtue he had picked up from his saintly grandmother Aaji that had stuck.

He hired this wrinkled black woman because she looked dirt-poor sitting by herself under the tree. It didn't matter in the least that she could speak only Tamil. He squatted over the baked orange earth and waited for her to tell him he would have sons, get rich, travel to exotic places, whatever. Three women, an old man, and a few curious urchins gathered around to watch. The man said he knew a little Marathi, Kiran's native tongue, and would translate.

"What did she say?" Kiran asked with a look of impatience.

The man looked uneasy and waggled his head side to side. He looked around him as if asking for help.

"It's OK. You can tell me. What did she say?"

"She said – she said you will – you will die in India, Sah'b," said the man through a nervous grin.

Kiran thought he heard wrong. "*What* did she say?"

"That you will die in India, Sah'b," said the man, still smiling.

"'Die,' you said?"

"Yes, Sah'b. That is what she said." He laughed nervously and looked around at the others for confirmation. One of the women said something, and they grinned as if at a joke. Then the man said, "We die in India, too!" They laughed a jittery laugh and looked back up at Kiran.

"Ask her when."

The man muttered something to the soothsayer, but she only shook her head and stared up at Kiran with her strangely bright, lashless, diseased eyes.

Kiran was anything but superstitious, but in the Madras airport he couldn't help but feel a little anxious. A terrorist had blown up thirty people there a few years back, and the Tamil Tigers across the straits in Sri Lanka were fighting for independence as doggedly as ever. Now, sitting comfortably in the plane, he couldn't help feeling relieved at the thought he would go on living a little longer.

For a long time Kiran had wanted to take a break from the usual grind of an academic philosopher pumping out one scholarly article after another, and write a novel. But about what? It had come to him one morning as he showered. In his Catholic days at Georgetown he felt a kinship with St. Thomas, the great doubter. According to legend Thomas sailed across the Indian Ocean to convert India to Christianity and was eventually martyred near Madras. Two thousand years later he was the patron saint of India's Catholics and was as loved and revered as Jesus. But Kiran had the idea of making *his* Thomas convert *away* from Christianity. Where did this idea come from? Under the spell, at sixteen, of a charismatic Jesuit at St. Xavier's in Bombay, he had done the unthinkable: converted to Catholicism. It had horrified and scandalized his high-caste Hindu family. So now he would, in a manner of speaking, atone. But Hinduism with all its deities wasn't anymore to his liking now than Christianity. So what would his Thomas convert to? To Buddhism, of course, the only religion that an atheist like himself could respect even a little. So this time Kiran found himself in India to do research on his novel, not just to visit his old mother.

He pushed his seat back and closed his eyes. Random memories started to come. Ravi looking out over Yosemite Valley after a strenuous father-and-son hike, spring rains in the Connecticut woods when he and Lisa were dating, warm moonlit nights on the Arabian Sea as seen from his bedroom window when he was a boy – they were such lovely memories. But there was also Shalini, his first love – too terrible to think about. He thought of how he used to feel after he made love to Lisa and lay awake staring at the ceiling; the libido had subsided, the passion had died; and he would find himself thinking of – Shalini. He went still further back in time and remembered how he felt called to the priesthood when he was at Georgetown. But in graduate school while studying philosophy he rebelled, turned his back on Catholicism, and locked into what the Church termed a worldly, materialistic track. He forgot all about a priestly vocation. Yet all those memories left a trace in his heart, like the faintly visible track of a snail.

He was jolted out of his reverie by a sari-clad stewardess serving him tea and a snack. He tore open the cellophane protecting his crackers and ate them, each in one bite.

He pushed his seat back again and closed his eyes. Turning his mind to his work, he congratulated himself. Everything had gone smoothly. He had interviewed ordinary Christians in Kerala and traveled up and down the coast where he meant to stage a debate between Thomas and a Buddhist sage. He traveled on a rickety bus over potholed roads to the village of Venni and snapped pictures of the battleground where King Karikal defeated enemy kings almost two thousand years ago, when Thomas might conceivably have been present.

And who would have thought there would be days left over for carefree travel? Kanchipuram, Tiruchchirapalli, Srirangam, Tanjore – their great temples, their undiluted Hinduism, the real India, the India he had rejected but still felt drawn to. He was glad he didn't go home early. The real India . . . his India . . .

". . . not ready to leave this world. If I died now, I would have to come back." An Indian's voice speaking British English with a Tamil accent woke Kiran out of his nap.

"But you are sure you come back?" said another voice in the unmistakable accent of an Eastern European struggling with English. "I am – how you say? – atheist" (he pronounced it "ah-tee-ist"), "so I not believe that."

They were sitting directly behind Kiran.

3

"I believe we keep coming back until we are free of the Great Illusion. Then there is eternal life," said the Indian.

There was something about this point of view that triggered in Kiran a faint, suppressed, nostalgic longing for the fruits of a living faith. He was hardly aware of it as he eavesdropped, but it was there anyway. "And you want eternal life?" said the other man.

"Yes and no; I want it, but not yet."

"You should be born Russian like me! Then you are not ashamed for your – your desire, heh heh heh!"

Kiran got up to go to the toilet and scanned the passengers as he walked back. Among them were a beautiful Tamil woman with a red bindi on her forehead and a long-lashed baby boy in her lap; a bloated man with weary, sagging features whom he took for an American; and a distinguished looking Muslim traveling with a woman whose face was veiled except for her eyes. The Russian, he decided, looked like Gorbachev.

Back in his seat, Kiran couldn't resist turning around and stealing another look at the beautiful Tamil madonna. She absent-mindedly kissed her baby on the head, and Kiran found himself thinking again of Shalini. He erased the image, and a picture of Lisa holding Sonya when she was a baby flashed across his memory. He looked again at the madonna loving her baby and again thought of Lisa holding Sonya. They were real. Shalini was not. Why did he feel so wretched?

His thoughts gravitated back to the conversation between the Indian and the Russian, and he realized clearly for the first time he had been rooting for the Indian. He wondered how this could be since he, like the Russian, was an atheist. Did he, Kiran Kulkarni, really want eternal life? Or did the wish arise like swamp gas out of some ancient, mouldering catacomb in his brain? *Interesting,* he noted.

By now the plane was more than halfway to Bombay, and the bright orange ball of a sun threatened to dive beneath the unbroken clouds below – when it happened. There was a faint thud. It barely registered on Kiran's consciousness. A minute later the door to the cockpit swung open and a crewman asked in English with peculiar urgency, "Is there a doctor here?"

"Yes, I am a doctor," said an old man off to Kiran's right. The man got up as everyone in the compartment stared in surprise. At that moment Kiran remembered the odd thud. Had anyone else felt it? "What happened?" he asked the crewman in an undertone. "I thought I felt – or heard something."

"A minor accident," the crewman said. But his face, which showed tiny pocks of blood like buckshot on the right side, was puffy, and his eyes seemed dazed.

"What kind of accident?"

The crewman ignored Kiran and held his arms out toward the doctor while his foot held the door ajar. "Come! Come!" he urged.

Kiran bent his body to the right and look through the unguarded passageway leading into the cockpit. A crewman with hands over his eyes and dripping blood was being propped up in the pilot's seat. Another man was frantically looking through a toolbox on the floor. Then Kiran saw twisted metal; some of the dials on the instrument panel were shattered.

"A bomb?" he whispered in shocked disbelief to the crewman as he led the doctor into the passageway.

"Nothing to worry about!" the crewman called back in a shrill, chastising whisper.

Then Kiran heard from the cockpit, "Bombay approach, this is Indian Airlines Flight one seven four, come in, over."

The door shut.

A bomb! Kiran felt a jab of terror. *What the hell!* No, he must stay cool. "Nothing to worry about," he remembered the man had said. And probably there wasn't. But his next thoughts were very different. They were those of a realist who has made a successful career of seeing things precisely as they are. *The clever bastard! It had to be someone on the inside, a mechanic maybe. Why didn't he just blow the whole damned plane up? I can't even smell smoke. The instrument panels, the controls – one lousy little plastic bomb. Nothing but a little glass in the face. Shit! –*

Kiran stuck his head in front of the dozing man on his left and looked back through the window at the engines. He saw nothing out of the ordinary, and the engines' steady purr told him they were running normally. *Nothing to fear, nothing to fear,* he told himself.

"Fasten your safety belts, extinguish all cigarettes, pull your trays into the upright position" – it was a man's voice, first in English, then in Tamil, then in Hindi. The muscles around Kiran's chest began to quiver. He told himself the instructions were just a precaution, but he wasn't sure. The intercom was working, and that at least was a good sign. He reminded himself that for every crash there are a hundred, perhaps a thousand close calls.

Meanwhile the passengers in first class were appealing to the two stewardesses who were hurrying up and down the aisle with towels in their hands. "What happened? What happened?" they said.

"... mayday, mayday. Bombay approach, this is Indian Airlines one seven four with an emergency, over."

Whoosh went the door as it shut.

A mayday! This couldn't be happening! thought Kiran. But it was happening. As a very young man he had always prayed on takeoff that the plane would not crash. He felt the old urge, but there was no one to pray to.

Then his thoughts started tumbling one over the other: *Indians can fix anything, we're geniuses at fixing things! My broken shoe, the cobbler on Mount Road in Madras, the hundred little tools spread out around him on the ground. Three minutes, two rupees, good as new! And that tool-box in the cockpit. Indians can fix anything. . . .* He thought of Ravi – he saw his serious face lighting up a little as he got off the plane and little Sonya's shiny curls and heard her delighted greeting, "Dad-*dee!*" with the accent on the second syllable. Son and daughter, so real, so alive, so young – only thirteen and eight. Surely they were a part of his future! They had to be.

The leper he gave twenty rupees to, the little dune of mud in Venni where cobras lived and were placated with prayer, the Christian fishermen of Tangasseri who took him out in their fishing boat, his office at school with the pictures of his children neatly mounted on his desk, Aaji, his parents, Lisa, Shalini, the, the – like Dracula in his black cape she loomed up batlike: the palm-reader in Kanchipuram! The words "You will die in India" dug into his brain, and he quietly screamed out a mighty *NO!* to any and all higher powers, real or unreal. *It was impossible! Impossible that she could be right! How could she know!*

The door to the cockpit opened. Man in a uniform.

"Sir!" Kiran said, fighting his panic.

The man pretended not to hear and rushed by.

Kiran almost unlatched his seatbelt to run after the man. He imagined himself grabbing the man's arm, spinning him around, and saying, "We have the right to know what's happened! We have the right to know if we're going to die!" He imagined the man falling back and then slithering away beyond the curtain into second class.

But Kiran only sat paralyzed in his seat.

Then he stared at the door separating the cockpit from the passengers and imagined himself barging through and demanding an explanation: *Either you tell them what has happened or I tell them. I know there's been an explosion, I know you've radioed a mayday. The people*

6

in second class don't know anything. They have a right to know. I have a right to know. Either you tell them or I tell them!

At that moment Kiran cared not even a little about the people in second-class. He wanted to know if he, Kiran Kulkarni, was going to die. That was all.

Voice over the intercom: "This is the co-pilot. There has been a small explosion in the cockpit and we are experiencing technical difficulties with the wing elevators." There was muttering and a few gasps. "You must stay calm," ordered the voice. "Keep your seatbelts fastened. Obey all instructions from the stewardesses. We are doing everything we can to regain control. We have time. Still – you should prepare yourselves."

The nose of the plane was tilted downward.

Now there were screams. Or rather wails. The veiled Muslim woman took up the death knell – her own! Her cries provided an unbroken background to the spasmodic shrieks and oaths of panic. Her voice was like the tambura which, when strummed, hums the sound of the eternal *Om*.

Could this be it? thought Kiran. *Could it really?* He thought of little Sonya and wondered how she would take it when – it was too horrible a thought! She needed him. And Ravi. The thought of his children being raised by Lisa alone – *no, it couldn't happen! It mustn't!*

A new sound, ugly, ridiculous. "A million dollars to anyone who can bring us home. A million dollars U.S.!" It was a shrill, gravelly shellburst belonging to someone stupefied with terror. "GODDAM IT! I WON'T DIE!" it exploded.

Kiran looked back in horror at the American. Who was he talking to, this man who sat chained to his seat, catatonic, rigid, shaking violently, screaming about his million dollars, like someone in the electric chair? Who was he talking to as he stared into space? Meanwhile the plane had tilted more severely downward toward the clouds, and the sun forced out its last rays before it sank behind the gray curtain.

For a moment an eerie quiet filled the cabin.

God, forgive me, Kiran heard an alien voice inside him say. *Quiet, you coward!* another voice answered. *Die by your convictions! Die as you have lived!* He repeated the words, *Die as you have lived,* again and again, like a mantra. *God, forgive me,* repeated the ancient, alien voice inside him.

For an instant he despised himself, then he took the matter in hand. He exhumed the long, complicated train of thought that had killed

God twenty years ago. Piece by piece, argument by argument, plank by plank he reviewed it, with unbelievable speed. He saw the inescapable conclusion – Therefore God does not exist – blazing like a laser beam into an endless Void. He heard the voice of Lucretius: *Nothing to fear.* The actual moment all there is to fear, then it's over, over. Just peaceful sleep, everlasting sleep of nothingness. Nothing to fear, nothing to fear. Then some other voice inside him said the whole argument was a worthless trick of the mind. He heard the voice of the old family priest down in Goa, saw the black temple idol of Kala Bhairava, the Lord of Time, that the priest worshipped. "I play with Him all day long," the old man had once said. *Oh Shiva!* an alien voice hidden very deep within Kiran cried out.

Then he heard a voice not in his own head, but behind him. "Teach me your God," said the Russian behind him to the Indian. "What I must do at this moment?"

"You must think only of God at the moment of death."

"But what is this God?"

"Infinite truth, infinite consciousness, infinite bliss," the voice carefully intoned like a bishop celebrating High Mass.

And infinite love, that ancient voice inside Kiran mocked.

He looked back down the aisle. There was the beautiful woman with the wide-eyed child in her lap. The child was sucking his thumb, unaware, content. The mother's face was upraised, her eyes closed, her lips moving.

He looked at the seat behind her. There was the American. His arms rigidly grasped the arms of his seat. He looked like someone in a dentist's chair when the drill has struck a nerve. He too had closed his eyes. A hundred wrinkles creased his flaccid, sweaty face. Had he too found a prayer, a means of deliverance? Would he be the good thief on the cross? *Him? Spare us!* Kiran screamed into the Void.

The Muslim. He was droning some tract in Urdu. He was calm, as if he had long ago prepared himself for just this.

All through the cabin the various names of God – Shiv, Ganesh, Krishna, Dev, Allah – could be heard; not in chant, but in fitful, fervent, frightened ejaculations.

The plane was now pointed more steeply downward toward the vast cloud bank, which lay like a thick pall between Kiran and extinction. Suddenly he hated the man who planted the bomb. He hated him because he didn't blow the plane up into smithereens and save everyone all this agony, this hypocrisy. And because his novel about Thomas would never get written. And because, because – it was unthinkable – he would never see his children again!

Kiran looked wildly around one last time. All these Hindus, Muslims, and Sikhs united in one simple thought. A stupendous superstition guaranteed to deliver them safely into the presence of God or a better next life. The Indian behind him had spoken of the Great Illusion. *But they're the ones caught in illusion!* Kiran reminded himself, now unsure. He thought of his life in California, the values and dreams of the gifted set he ran with. And he asked himself what was real, this or that? He wasn't sure. He really didn't know. He wondered if he had made some – some preposterous miscalculation.

He looked out the window at a break in the clouds. Three minutes? His brain exploded with preternatural energy. Heaped layers of images broke out of their prison, and he saw them all simultaneously. He heard and saw bamboo stalks creaking in the wind, crashing into each other, scarring each other. He heard the haunting whoops of the koël set off against crows' caws. He saw monsoon clouds racing each other to the northeast, the ones overhead scudding faster than those more distant. He tasted the bitter leaf of the margosa tree and saw birds riding on the rumps of cattle. India rushed by in a hundred images, none excluded. Then events out of the more distant past began to vie for space, and, as before, nothing was excluded. He was an amazed but helpless spectator as he relived Sonya's birth, his seminar philosophy classes at Columbia University, the ecstasy he felt listening to a classical concert with his friends when he was just a teenager, the high ceilings of his grand ancestral home, the little snub-nosed girl he gave candy to in first standard, his dear mother when he was a toddler–

"This is the pilot speaking!" Kiran jumped in his seat. "Prepare for a possible crash landing. Lower your head behind the seat in front of you. And God be with you." In three languages the pilot spoke these absurd words. Two-hundred fifty bodies crouched down. There was the sound of rustling, then some whimpering, but mostly an astonishing quiet.

Now Kiran saw himself from a new angle. Systematically he had pumped all spiritual convictions out of himself. His soul was like the vacuum inside a light bulb or a TV tube, and the materialism and worldliness that had vitrified around him were like the shell, the glass of the tube. He realized he hated what he had become even as he knew there was no turning back.

He reached for his briefcase, opened it, ripped off a cover of a hard-back book on temple architecture, and scribbled on the inside with a quivering hand, "Lisa, thinking of you and kids. Will in third drawer on left. Munja for Ravi. Munja, yes! So sorry, so sorry. Love, K." He closed the briefcase full of notes, books, undeveloped film, and the hardback book cover.

The steeply tilted plane hit the clouds and vibrated as if it would disintegrate before it hit the ground. People whimpered, prayed, but mostly there was just quiet. Suddenly, as the plane lurched, Kiran glimpsed a gray landscape out the window. He unbuckled his seat belt, reared up, and leaned over: a perverse commitment to realism, a lifelong habit, compelled him to see what death looked like as it zoomed toward him. It looked like a millet field. He whipped himself back against his seat and tried to dissolve in it. He couldn't find one end of his seat belt. What did it matter? He made his body rigid, as if bracing himself against impact, and squeezed his eyes shut. He waited for that precise moment, that millisecond between consciousness and oblivion. The words *Oh God!* rushed at him pleading and begging and screaming, but he cut them off. In their place he substituted a memory of Ravi as he kicked the winning goal in the last seconds of a child's soccer game in California. On Ravi's face there had been a smile that lit up the universe. It was the happiest moment that father and son had ever known together. Now Kiran clung to that smile, clung to that smile. With a violent, flashing, pulverizing crash, the Void closed round.

Kiran looked upon a fiery, smoky scene. As if to make sure he was still alive, he ran his hands over his chest. He felt his shirt, felt that it was open at the collar. It was amazing. He was intact, he was unhurt! He studied the fuselage of the burning plane in the millet field, the charred bodies, most still strapped in their seats, the peasants running up; he heard the shrieks of the women, and his amazement only grew. Then he remembered he hadn't been able to fasten his seatbelt. Had he been thrown free? Yes, that must be it. Now rescuers were all around, and he tried to tell them that everyone was dead – except himself. But they took no notice of him; it was as if he wasn't even there. And then one of them – one of them walked right through him. Even then he didn't understand. Not at first. But when it happened a third time, the truth blasted him with its full – was it horror? At one level it was. He realized that all the fools of the world had been right after all and that he, the philosopher – how could it be? No, it couldn't. But it was. There couldn't have been any survivors, so he must be among the dead. Yet here he was. His next thought was that he was cut off from his children and his friends. No, he must not let himself think of them, not now. Again he marveled that he was still a conscious, living being. He could even smell the burned bodies. With what? A nose? Back on earth he hadn't the slightest doubt that all that was happening to him was absolutely impossible.

Why wasn't he elated? He had cheated death, yet he felt edgy, almost panicky. Ravi and Sonya. *Oh my God! Oh my God!* he repeated over and over as the truth sank in. He would never see them again. And they would never see him. *Oh my God!* It was too horrible to think about.

It began to grow darker, and he had no idea where he was supposed to go or what was supposed to happen. He was lost; he was alone. It occurred to him that there might be a hell, that most impossible of all fictions. After all, wouldn't he have to pay for his error? Justice and condemnation – didn't he deserve to suffer? There certainly wasn't a welcoming committee! In his loneliness he suddenly found himself thinking of Shalini, almost hoping that she might turn up. Where might she be in this strange world that death couldn't reach? Then a heaviness came over him, and all he wanted to do was lie down on the spot and go to sleep forever.

Chapter 2

KIRAN had left Lisa a copy of his itinerary, and the day and destination of the crashed Indian Airlines plane matched. She turned off the news and steadied herself. She knew it was possible Kiran had changed his plans, but unlike many people in her predicament who would hope against the most desperate odds, she tried to convince herself that Kiran was dead. It wasn't that she really believed he was, but she wanted to be prepared just in case. She was a Lewis, a Daughter of the American Revolution, and an Anglican, even if she hadn't been to church in eight years and hadn't even bothered to get Sonya baptized. If necessary she would cope much better than Kiran or anybody else suspected. She picked up the newspaper and tried to read.

It was 10:40 in the morning when the call came to the Connecticut home where she grew up and where she and the children were vacationing with her mother and step-father. Sonya was two houses down playing with a friend. Siggy, the Burmese cat, was stretched out at the foot of the bed, its belly turned upward. Lisa with her third cup of coffee was reading *The New York Times*, every page of it, even the sports section. Usually she never glanced at the sports, which was Kiran's domain, but on this particular morning she looked at the baseball scores. That is what she was doing when the phone rang.

As soon as she hung up, Lisa realized she had never really believed Kiran was on the plane. In spite of her carefully cultivated stoicism, the idea was simply unacceptable, so she was shocked when the voice on the phone was not Molly's or Barbara's. The man held out hope: he said it was night in India and that no one knew yet how bad it was. He said the plane had crashed in the vicinity of some unpronouncable place and that rescue operations had begun. He said he was sorry.

Two days later the bag with Kiran's body in it – what was left of it – arrived at a crematorium in Bombay.

Lisa had wanted the body buried, but she was no match for his family. The obsequies would be Hindu, the body cremated, the ashes scattered. Lisa would be on the next flight.

On an Air India jumbo jet, Lisa sat next to her mother, Velma Stein. The children, silent and numb, sat on the other side of the aisle. Like many patrician New Englanders, Velma said either too little about death or too much. For the last two days she hadn't alluded in any way to Kiran's death; they might as well have been going down to India as tourists. But on the plane after a second scotch-and-water she began to complain to Lisa about her third husband, Pavlov, who was eighty-five.

"Pavy is a little ga-ga, you know. If only" – she suddenly leaned over close to Lisa and lowered her voice – "if only he had the courage to take the pills. I've left them with him, but he just won't take them. I've reminded him of our agreement that if one of us ever became incontinent . . . why can't he be honest, modern, and realistic?"

When saying something controversial, Velma would jerk her hands outward or upward as she talked, as if she were offhandedly throwing poisoned darts behind her back. There was a droll, coquettish quality about her voice which at once suggested she was only a naughty girl of seventyish who should not be taken too seriously and an absolute monarch entitled to say whatever she damn well pleased however outrageous. Over the years Lisa had watched her mother casually impale both friend and enemy alike, so she should not have been shocked. But she was. After all, Pavy was her husband. Was there no limit to what the woman would say? Remnants of a poem about "decent, godless people remembered for their one hundred lost golf balls" rippled through her mind from somewhere – she had no idea where. Besides, Mother wasn't decent. Behind her theatrical smile was venom.

"I mean it's obvious," Velma went on, "that this is the only life there is. And when it goes bad –"

"Mother, how can you be so sure? Maybe Pavy isn't sure. Maybe that's what keeps him from doing it. Mother, sometimes you appall me!"

The two women were quiet for a few minutes, but then Velma, as she finished off her scotch-and-water, brought up Kiran. "How do you feel about Kiran's ashes being thrown into a river? I mean, there's not even a place for the children to remember him."

"My God, Mother, must we talk about it? Of course I don't like it!"

"India. Of all places to end up," said Velma, again trying to be droll, her nicotine-rusty vocal chords purring.

"That's where he came from, Mother!"

"Don't be touchy, dear, I was only trying to cheer you up." Velma quieted a moment, then asked, "Then what *are* your objections to India?"

"India's not really the problem. It's *anyplace* that's so far away from his friends, though he really didn't have many to speak of, and – and us. Nobody will *be* there."

"And then there's this Hindu business," added Velma.

"That doesn't bother me. It's religion in general that bothers me; KK had put it all behind him."

"But Hindus – they are so – so, so, so *superstitious*," said Velma. "And they really take the next world seriously. Rebirth and all that other rot. I mean they really *believe* in it. Not like our Father Tom."

"But KK *was* a Hindu, Mother. And how can you be so sure they aren't right? . . . I *hope* they are, don't you?"

"Really, Lisa, you need to see a good psychiatrist."

Lisa was boiling, but she held her tongue. Mother, after all, was seventy-two, and although she wouldn't admit it, everyone knew she was an alcoholic – she had always been one. The irony was that Pavy had a good deal more of his wits left than she.

"But let's suppose they're right," Velma said. "Your husband – I find it hard to say his name – was selfish and cruel. He lived for his work and reputation. Nothing came before that. He didn't give a damn about you. And he had no time for his children."

"You don't know what you're talking about, Mother!" Lisa hissed.

"Keep your voice down. The children will hear you."

"He would have *killed* for his children. Killed, I tell you. He adored them. And he was brilliant. If anyone had a good excuse to neglect his children – "

"But you said yourself he neglected them – "

"You know how I complain! Yeah, he was a workaholic, and we didn't have the best of marriages. But – "

"He was a bastard, and you know it! A snotty, brown-faced bastard! You said as much yourself! And if you're right about another life, I can tell you right where he is. Hell was made for the likes of him!"

"Oh my God!" Lisa sobbed, covering her face with her hand. "Drop it, Mother!"

"He looked down on us. You called him 'His Majesty.' He looked down on *me!* Can you imagine? Who did he think he was?"

And with that, Velma Stein at last held her peace.

Still sobbing, Lisa took several deep breaths and calmed herself.

"What's *wrong*, Mom?" said Sonya from across the aisle. "Mo-om?!"

"Nothing. Just – just missing – I'll be all right."

Lisa finally calmed herself, then turned her thoughts to Kiran.

Mother's right, KK. You were a bastard. But I loved you! She felt the familiar rage starting to boil. *If you'd just listened to me! But you just had to go write that novel. A novel, you, the great philosopher! You just had to go to that shithole country and – and get yourself killed and – and desert us. For a novel! What were you thinking? God, what am I going to do? What am I going to do with Ravi? He's so sullen. I can't get him to open up. O Kiran, I'm so sorry. I'm so sorry for everything, for everything. Kiran . . . I . . . I . . .*

Three weeks later Kiran's scuffed, scorched briefcase arrived in the mail, and Lisa found his last words scribbled on the book cover. By then she was already back in California readying affairs for the move back east. She had dug out her nursing manuals and already lined up a job in Old Saybrook. The note on the jacket of the book left her numb – except for the final request. *Munja? Munja?* she said to herself over and over. She knew that Munja meant the Sacred Thread Ceremony. But he had discarded his own thread long ago, when he converted to Catholicism as a teenager. *What could it mean?* she wondered. *What happened to him on the plane? Did the son of a bitch get religion? Munja?* She read the scribbled message again and again and marveled. She started laughing. *So the son of a bitch got religion!* She found the thought hilarious. It was as if he had been the butt of a very undignified joke. She laughed violently, her sides splitting. Then, without warning, she began to cry. She knew how he adored the children and felt sorry for him. And Sonya was still crying herself to sleep. Even at the end he was thinking of them. She really did love the son of a bitch, and she took a secret solace and found a strange peace in his last pious instruction, which she fully intended to carry out.

Six weeks after Kiran's ashes were sprinkled over the Mandovi River in Goa and his spirit set free, Ravi recited the *Gayatri Mantra* and received the sacred thread at a simple Hindu temple ceremony in New York.

Chapter 3

KIRAN found himself somewhere in the Bronx not far from Fordham University – or so it seemed. Wasn't this his old graduate school neighborhood? Like a bloodhound on the trail of some warm wounded animal, he had only one thought, one wish. It dominated him as he wound his way back and forth up the unlit stairwell toward the fifth floor where she lived. He hadn't even bothered to call ahead to see if she was there; somehow he knew she was. And he also knew, as he pressed the doorbell, that she was waiting for him.

She came to the door in her soft light green dress, a simple, thin one-piece mini of soft polyester that exposed her smooth, shapely legs well above the knee. It was "his" dress, the one they had bought together from Macy's on a dare and that she wore exclusively for him in her apartment. He feasted his eyes on those legs as they glided ahead of him into the warm living room and quickly crossed themselves on the couch facing him where he stood.

"Sit down, darling," she said. Her dark eyes scanned him with obvious pleasure. "Would you like me to put some music on?"

"You choose," he said.

She put on Mozart's *Clarinet Quintet* and sank gracefully back onto the couch. Her wonderful legs and firm, upright little breasts stuck out at him, and he knew that Shalini still belonged to him absolutely. He had only to – but why rush? Her undistinguished but sensitive face, the face he had rejected in favor of Lisa's aristocratic glamor, was exactly the same as he remembered it. And he was glad of this, he celebrated it – celebrated every square centimeter of it.

"Shally, it's so good to *see* you again like this!"

"I've waited an eternity for this," she said softly, her eyes glowing with long pent-up excitement.

Everything was exactly as it had been when they were graduate students, except that now they did not speak of theology or Sylvia Plath, the focus of her research just before she died. They were living on an astral planet but knew nothing of it. Dreams of earth shut all that out and clasped them to its bosom. It was as if they had simply rediscovered each other after a long separation, like long lost lovers who happen to stumble across each other in a strange city. Shalini told Kiran she had finally "forgiven" him and since that day had been preparing for their "everlasting reunion." Kiran was so happy to be with her again in the old way that not even the word "everlasting" ruffled him. The music she played for him, both on the stereo and on her cello, was the same she played for him back on earth.

Slowly, on that first day together, she drew him to her. She poured him a glass of mango lassi and served him a delicious meal of chapati-bhaaji, with kheer for dessert, just as he had taught her to do so long ago. She delighted him with her innocent but strangely canny observations. But most of all she wooed him with soft touches as she passed back and forth across the room, with quick little glances that communicated a kind of girlish shyness mixed somehow with a leonine hunger, and with the soft, dizzy swaying of the green dress around hips and buttocks that were round, compact, and utterly exciting.

The dirty windows rattled under the battering of the cold wind as they climbed into bed, but the sound was like music to their long-chastened ears. She made him glory in his body just like in the old days, except that every sensation was heightened and protracted beyond anything he remembered. He lay prostrate as her hands and fingers worked faithfully, lovingly, adoringly over every pore, teasing him, enticing him. He was besotted with pleasure when she stopped at last and gave him the quiet signal with her glowing eyes. Slowly he undressed her, took off the soft dress, kissed her lips and neck, let his hands wander across her body, leading her, thrilling her. She became consumed with desire and could not wait for him. She squirmed out of her panties and fell on him with a frantic passion. She made him feel that he was a man, a whole man; but not just a man, a king; but not just a king, a god. He was no longer in a one-bedroom flat somewhere in the Bronx on a sleety January day; he was in paradise.

Like lions gorging themselves far beyond the point of satiety after a particularly large kill, Kiran and Shalini gorged themselves on the sweet fat of sex. Hour after hour, day after day they cavorted and primped, teased and laughed, rubbed and scratched, sucked and cleaved. They found a copy of the *Kama Sutra* and practiced the various positions. They looked into each other's faces and saw passion welling up under the skin, saw unrepletable desire fixing the eyes in a drugged stare. They became oblivious to everything but the oblivion of the art they practiced.

Gradually their dalliances grew monotonous, and they began snapping at each other, each unconsciously blaming the other for the waning of desire, for the failure to play the role of an endlessly pleasing god or goddess. They began noticing the weather, looking at television, reading the paper. They went out shopping, made plans to go to Europe, talked to mothers strolling their babies, talked about having a baby of their own.

One night as Kiran lay in bed waiting for Shalini to get finished in the bathroom, almost dreading still another act of sex but knowing he would go through with it, he felt a call of distress reaching him from some unknown place. Someone seemed to be calling out to him, missing him, angry about something.

Kiran's attention riveted on the caller. He felt himself being drawn into some kind of a mist, a clammy darkness with vague, menacing presences hovering around him. Then he saw a fuzzy light, a tunnel of indistinct light that looked like the full moon seen through lifting fog. He got closer and closer to the light until he saw figures. There was the caller, a boy. He was pacing, his face was troubled, his brow creased and his eyes red and angry. That face! Suddenly Kiran understood that the boy belonged to him. It was his son, it was Ravi!

He felt Ravi's anger and understood it was directed at the woman, his mother. There she was, in the next room, the bedroom. There was a man in bed with her, a man younger than her. Even in his sluggish state Kiran recognized Lisa and knew she was his wife and this was their bedroom. He wanted to protest, to —

"Kiran, what's wrong!"

Kiran heard the voice like a gong struck at his ear. It came from another dimension, and he fell back into it. He looked up at Shalini hovering over him in bed. He felt confusion and disgust. What was he doing here with Shalini while that man, that young crotch-smeller, was in bed with his wife? He got up and began looking for his clothes.

"I've got to get over there!" he said.

"Where?" said Shalini.

"Home. I'm going to catch her in the act, that slut!"

"Kiran, what are you talking about? *This* is home!"

"This? What do you mean?" He looked at her incredulously.

"Do you mean you'd *still* rather be with her?"

A look of confusion and guilt clouded Kiran's face.

"You . . . you . . . you'd rather be with *her?*" she spluttered. "Kiran, you'd really rather be with that – that – ?! Look at me!" she yelled.

He looked away as he sat down naked on the edge of the bed. He was completely bewildered.

"After all we've been through? I can't believe it! Oh, when will it ever end? *When?*" She was wailing at the ceiling: "*W-h-e-n? W-h-e-n?*" Over and over she wailed, her arms lifted like a beggar's. Tears slid down her cheeks onto her pink nightie.

But he hardly noticed her as he stood next to the bed and thought.

She stopped wailing and scrambled on her knees over the bed to where he stood."After all we've been through together!" She was shouting at him up close, her face contorted by fear, her eyes large and crazy with pain.

But he only half heard her as he watched her curl up on the bed below him. He almost asked her to explain, but then he remembered. He remembered that this woman, this despairing woman curled up on the bed, was the woman who killed herself over him a long time ago in some other world. Yes, this was the very same woman. But what was she doing here? How could she be in the same world as Lisa? What was going on? Where exactly *was* he? Then, in a flash, he remembered the plane crash; he saw it all, remembered it all. He had died. Yet now he was alive. He had been in one world, now he was in another. That was the starting point of his analysis. The philosopher in him woke.

The place where he now found himself looked just like Shalini's old apartment, but it couldn't possibly be. It existed on earth, but he existed somewhere else. Was he dreaming? No, he was wide awake. And out of his awakeness something strange began to happen.

"Shally, we've got to get out of here. It's a trap!"

"Don't talk to me! I despise you!"

"Shalini, this – we –"

"DON'T TOUCH ME!"

"This place isn't real! Don't you see? Look, it's dissolving! Right in front of our eyes, it's beginning to dissolve! It's something we've been projecting. It's some sort of illusion. I don't know. A shared hallucination. And we're getting out of it!"

"You're mad, Kiran! What are you babbling?"

"We've died, Shally! We've died! Don't you remember? This place isn't earth! Back on earth you had a cat. Remember Scherzo? You always had a cat. Scherzo was that adorable black cat you loved so much. Don't you remember telling me he was your best friend until I came along? You loved cats. Don't you remember?"

"What are you talking about? Scherzo is . . ." She looked around. "Scherzo!" she called. "SCHERZO!" But there was no Scherzo.

"Where is he, Shally? Look, the room's dissolving! It was a dream. And now we're waking up."

"What are you talking about? This is my *apartment!*"

Suddenly he was completely free of the illusion, and the last thing he heard was a pitiful wail, "Kiran, don't leave me, don't leave me! O, please, please, *please* don't leave me again! KIRAN. Kiran – " Her voice faded away like the whir of a spent gust of wind. It was the loneliest, most heartrending sound he had ever heard.

He found himself in a chilly mist surrounded by . . . he couldn't tell. Shapes were moving through the gloom. The air was close, stuffy. The shapes came and went, but he couldn't make them out. And no one spoke to him. He didn't know what to do, where to go. A terrible thought came to him, the thought that he was in hell. And out of that suspicion arose a wish so intense that it seemed to vibrate in the thick air. The wish was in fact a prayer, a prayer tossed out into the universe, to any god or goddess in the vicinity, for deliverance. It arose reflexively, but the next one, a repeat of the first, was intentionally chosen. It reflected a kind of faith – or a hope – in the possibility of some sort of rescue. And coming forth from that act, pouring out of that prayer as it were, was a light. In the distance Kiran noticed it. It grew bigger and seemed to be approaching him. It seemed to be heading straight for him. As it got closer, it felt welcoming. And then it was upon him, enveloping him, loving him. Yes, even loving him! It took him up, took him away from the barren twilight world that he'd been dumped into when the illusory earth dream broke up. Suddenly he knew exactly where he was, and he couldn't believe his eyes.

Chapter 4

THE Mandovi River just upstream from Panjim in Goa, the land of his ancestors – forested, lush, flowered – that is where he found himself overlooking water as blue as sapphire. The whole scene was so similar to his ancestral home back on earth that he had to remind himself over and over that he was really "dead." Even the house with its canopy of gulmohar trees bursting with flame-colored blossoms from top to bottom was a precise replica. It had been his favorite place on earth. A stiff breeze out of the southwest – at least that's what he would have called it back on earth – whipped the dancing astral water into frothy whitecaps. Looking back toward the house from the grassy terrace where he sat, he saw an enormous banyan tree dropping its aerial roots into a lawn fronting the villa. Jasmine trees with delicate white blossoms and mimosas with their pinks stood close up against the house, and acacias with tube-shaped yellow flowers spanned out left and right into jungle. A catamaran with a saffron sail billowing out in front leapt up the river. Kiran waved at a black-bodied man in a lungi captaining the boat, but the man did not see him.

As a boy he had spent many a day lounging on a deck chair or fishing or shelling crabs or reading or swimming or playing cards or chasing away a snake that had wandered onto this terrace. Where he found himself now had been constructed by a team of builders following the instructions of his paternal grandfather Ganesh. Aaji and Ganesh, as much husband and wife now as they had been on earth, never guessed they might have to share this home – this home so like earth, but not earth – with one of their grandchildren so soon.

It had been only a few hours since he woke from a long sleep following his earth dream. Now he was in a world called Eidos, and its beauty, its sheer *realness,* was stunning. Ganesh and Aaji invited him to stay with them rather than live in an apartment in Eidos' capital city, Vimala.

On the second day following his sleep, Kiran and Aaji sat on the verandah looking out over the river. She took his hand in hers, and as she looked into his eyes, he looked back into hers. What a brilliant being his dear old Aaji had become! Everything about her suggested intelligence, cheerfulness, good intent, youthful energy. Her eyes had a sparkling, honey-like transparency about them that made him think of an angel. They were set rather deeply under an upright, shiny forehead. Thick black hair framed her face in soft waves. Her cheekbones were high and rather pronounced, and her delicate mouth and fine, clean-cut jaw were nuanced by a high-minded nobility, but a nobility without arrogance. Her smile revealed regular white teeth – did she take these out at night and put them in a jar as she had done back on earth? He bet not. She was dressed in a glowing, almost dazzling robe of a color somewhere between blue and violet. She was much younger, even beautiful, younger in appearance even than he; yet she was still his dear granny who read Kipling aloud to him when he was a boy, taught him how to do the daily puja ritual, and in countless other ways loved him.

"I still can't – I still can't believe you're here," he said. "I can't tell you how amazed I am by this world, this Eidos – its incredible beauty."

Her eyes danced. She seemed immensely stimulated. "As you can tell, everything here is played an octave higher than anything on earth. My dear boy, what adventures lie ahead of you! If only we can keep you here!"

Keep me here? He looked at her face and thought he felt something like pity. *If only we can keep you here!* What did that mean? He felt a creepy sensation.

"Let's walk," she said.

As light as a feather, he got up. He was still not used to the way gravity worked.

They walked along a path next to the river. They didn't speak, just held hands. He gaped and marveled at a flowery meadow stretching away to his right. He felt a maternal compassion coming from Aaji. Then he became vaguely aware of a voice, a feeling, a presence from very far away, as if from the edge of the universe. Was it his imagination?

The voice intruded into his world like a tiny child tugging lightly at his pants to get attention.

What was this? It had the feel of Lisa. It grew in intensity. Then, like a Muslim prayer called out into the wind from a distant minaret, it faded away.

They walked on in silence for a few moments. "Hello down there!" a voice called out from above.

They looked up and saw a boy about twelve waving from high up inside a giant orange-pink flower shaped like a hibiscus that he had crawled into. Aaji waved back. "Having fun?"

"Oh yes," said two voices, and out popped another boy's head next to the first.

"I'm showing my grandson around; he's new here," Aaji chimed in. "Don't fall!"

The boys laughed as if at a good joke as grandmother and grandson walked on. "Did I miss something?" said Kiran.

"Spirits don't hurt themselves when they fall, that's all. It's one of our endless earth jokes."

"Really?" He digested what she said, then asked, "So sometimes gravity works, and sometimes it doesn't?"

"Oh, it always works! It's just that our bodies are so light and our minds so agile that we can overcome it at will, and with ease. Oh, Kiran! It's such fun to laugh at all those troubles we once took so seriously back on earth!"

As they walked on, he looked at Aaji and felt with a jolt of dismay that he was a nobody. He felt like he didn't belong in this beautiful but weird world Aaji called Eidos. Where *did* he belong? Was he really shivering, or did he just imagine it? He felt Aaji's reassuring grip, then remembered his children. He missed earth intensely, even missed Lisa.

He asked what sort of work he was expected to do in Eidos. Whatever it was, he was ready to start. He had to get his mind off earth.

"Not so fast," Aaji laughed. "Get your rest, gather your strength – you'll need it, a lot of it. It wasn't too long ago that your father and son sprinkled your ashes over earth's Mandovi. Learn to love this place, so like the place you loved back on earth. Love its frogs and geckos, its birds – do you remember how fascinated you were by the koël with its haunting call? Even the snakes that crawl in from the forest are friendly here. When a cobra rears up, it does so in greeting. Greet it back. You're a pigeon, and this is your dovecote. This is your anchor to Eidos. Try to avoid earth dreams like the one you shared with your old girl friend – they will tempt you, as they tempted most of us. They could even lead you, God forbid, to the Shadowlands for a long stay. That's where you were when you called out for help and Ganesh came to your rescue. Suppose you hadn't called out – " She seemed to shudder. "Avoid earth dreams *at all costs.*"

From time to time he thought about Shalini, and he asked Aaji if he would meet her again.

"Oh, yes – during Judgment, and possibly sooner," said Aaji. "There's a great deal of unfinished business there, isn't there?" She then added quietly, almost solemnly, with a scowl, "I'm sorry to say she's not doing well. She's still in her little apartment down in the Shadows, tightly shut up in her dream, afraid of what's outside. It's a pitiful situation. No one has been able to get through to her. Maybe someday you – but who knows?" Aaji slowed her walk and looked pensively out at the horizon. "I have a feeling . . . well, we'll just have to wait and see."

To pass the time – there was a lot of it – Kiran took to exploring his new world, trying to find comfort in it. He learned to project himself beyond the boundaries of Eidos into other astral realms – there were thousands of them! The sights fascinated him: the Eskimo snowscapes, the Amazon-like jungles of tribal peoples, the quaint medieval-looking towns of some of Italy's traditional Catholics, the misty mountainscapes of inland China's peasants, and hundreds of other ethnic or religious realms. Sometimes he would join other travelers, usually newcomers like himself. Sometimes they would see the sights from above – flying was no problem for him now – and sometimes at ground level. But usually he traveled alone. He drank in the sights. Ever curious back on earth, he satisfied his curiosity on this vast astral planet spreading out millions of miles in all directions from its dense center, earth. Fellow sojourners didn't bother to greet him unless he greeted them first. He felt accepted by everyone he met but loved by none.

The name "Grandpa Ganesh" had only a ghostly reality for Kiran growing up in Bombay. Ganesh had died of colon cancer at the age of fifty-two when Kiran's father was only thirteen. When Kiran was born in 1944, Ganesh's full-length picture hanging in the huge living room of the "big house" on Marine Drive had already darkened with age. Kiran had missed his paternal grandfather by fifteen years.

"A wonderful man" is the way Aaji described her husband to Kiran when he was a child back on earth. Now that he knew Ganesh, lived in the same house with him, he began to see that Aaji's praise grew out of more than family loyalty.

Ganesh looked to be about fifty – quite a bit older than most spirits – had a strong jaw, a deeply lined forehead over dark receptive eyes, and a full head of combed-back, unparted, gray-black hair. His hands were large and gentle, and his hairy arms were bare from the elbow as they reached out from beneath a loosely hanging, buttonless beige shirt that glowed with his unique auric signature. Everything about his appearance was masculine except his eyes, which radiated a kindly softness that Kiran at first associated with a woman's face. There was something about him that was definitely special.

Now it was time to explore his own realm, and Ganesh and Aaji were to be his guides. "Eidos is a unique realm for this level," Ganesh said. "It's a melting pot. Some would say it's a hodge-podge – of geographies and cultures and religions – or no religions. You'll find a little of everything here. You could say its central themes are variety and abundance. There are a lot of Indians here. After all, there are a lot of Indians, period!"

In its capital city, Vimala, twelve million souls worked and played. Aaji and Ganesh had been whetting Kiran's appetite for a visit there since he arrived, but he had always been reluctant to enter its strange, unnerving light, which he often viewed from high above as he passed overhead. Ganesh told him Vimala was "the universe's most beautiful city, even more beautiful than Judaica's capital, astral Jerusalem. Einstein and other physicists live there and are trying to unlock the mysteries of astral matter and light."

"Incredible!" said Kiran. "Do you know what kind of heresy such talk would be where I used to work? Everything is turned upside down here. This place isn't even supposed to exist, much less be a laboratory for a science the earth hasn't even dreamed of. It's almost as if the Universe is laughing at us!"

Aaji and Ganesh looked at each other and smiled.

Kiran's destination was the Hall of Records, where someday he would undergo the ordeal officially known as Judgment – and unofficially "the Trial," "the Torment," or "the Desert." They could arrive at the Hall in an instant by teleportation, but Aaji thought he would enjoy walking in and seeing the city, block by block. So the three of them walked up the great avenue toward the city center, where the Hall stood 366 stories high.

Vimala's main avenue was flanked by slender trees that reached as high as redwoods and flowering shrubs set in between. The first buildings stood smallish and rather plain, but they were always clean and neat, as in Switzerland. As they penetrated the city, he noticed how blocks of houses alternated with blocks of trees and parks. Ganesh explained that outlying districts of the city had been "torn down" a few earth years ago and "recreated" along the lines of a checkerboard. The "black" squares were green zones, the "red" were buildings. Botanical gardens full of birds singing notes of exquisite beauty stood in some of the black squares. Meadows with gurgling streams spread out invitingly in others. Still others had parks where citizens, mostly newcomers and children, played tag or gyrated their delightful astral bodies in ways unimagined on earth.

On one of the squares there were no trees, just a floormat of wildflowers stretching across the entire area. Above the floormat swarmed hundreds of children playing some kind of game.

"And these kids are what you might call orphans – they all existed on earth for a little while? I mean, they're not, you might say, *angels,* with no earth history?" said Kiran.

"That's right. You might call them orphans in reverse," said Aaji. "Their parents didn't die. *They* did."

Actually many games were going on side by side, stretching from one end of the square to the other. Kiran stopped and watched one of them. The field of play was three-dimensional, shaped like a shoebox, with height as well as length and width. The goals stood at opposite ends of the shoebox halfway between the floor and the ceiling, which were marked by a faint sheen of red "paint" you could see through. The players, all of them hovering above the ground, some upside down, others at a lean, attacked or defended the "net." They reminded Kiran of wasps, fifteen on a side. Mind met mind in an effort to control the flight of the ball. There wasn't any kicking, but there couldn't be any doubt that soccer or hockey was the inspiration behind the game.

"It's mostly a game for training children to use their minds to control matter," Ganesh explained. "They keep themselves aloft and control the ball, and that's a start. And it's great fun."

Kiran found himself thinking of Ravi and how he'd love this game. *Oh Ravi,* he sang in his heart. *Oh Ravi! What I'd give to have you here!*

The city's pedestrians usually walked out of habit, but many glided just above the avenue without moving their legs. A few even flew overhead or vaulted off the surface to see something or "hopped" high to avoid another pedestrian. Others simply vanished when they decided midway to reach their destination in a hurry. Children often rode on the backs of animals, and when they fell off, they laughed and hopped back on unhurt. The broad avenue that headed toward the Great Temple standing at the city center wasn't so much a street as a scenic corridor as wide as a football field, its surface made of rich green grass as soft as moss. Cars and buses and trucks didn't travel over it – you could find these only in one of Eidos's many earth museums. In a space where everything could be created by one's imagination and will, including one's own body, nothing needed to be hauled or transported.

As they approached Vimala's center, the quality of the light changed. Impossible to describe with the vocabulary of earth, it seemed to radiate from the 400-story Temple, its heaven-reaching spire surrounded by light stretching upward indefinitely into dark blue space. To the right of the Temple stood a humbler but still massive satellite, the multicolored Hall of Records, and to the left the "Silo," a towering windowless coal-black cylindrical building, beautiful in its own stark way, that symbolized the human womb. If the great avenue on which the threesome walked could be thought of as the nave of a prodigious cathedral, then the Temple flanked by the Hall of Records and the Silo would be its transept. How small the imagination of earth! Kiran thought. How impecunious her achievements! He thought of people back on earth who envied their friends living in places like San Francisco and Santa Barbara, and smiled.

The closer they got to the Temple, the more splendid the architecture became. Amphitheaters abounded; rain and dust and cold didn't exist in the capital. At every corner there stood some piece of sculpture, some Rodin-like masterpiece of astral face or form, or some exuberant expression of geometric shape more complex and fascinating than any earth had to show. Flowers in boxes suspended outside windows draped the sides of buildings. At intersections soaring granite-like monoliths served as palettes for Eidos' master artists. Everywhere there was vivid color and fascinating form. The architecture was more European than Indian, but the colors of the buildings made one think of a sari. The blacks and beiges and cloudy silvers so stylish in America were eclipsed by bright colors everywhere. There was cheer, or attempts at cheer, all around.

They walked on, and light poured down in ever greater purity as they got closer to the Temple.

"How do you feel?" Aaji said.

"Strange. There is something about the light that makes me feel, well, dizzy. It's almost too awe-inspiring for me. Do I belong here?"

"Now you see why every realm has its Shadowlands. If even you feel this, imagine – "

"Maybe I belong in the Shadowlands on a permanent basis, Aaji! Maybe I'm not ready for this."

"You? No, no. You've come too far for that. You just got lost for a little while. Anyway, let's see how you feel when we – "

"What's that?" Kiran broke in. He pointed up at what looked like a mermaid gliding through the air headfirst, as if fishtailing her way through an unseen ocean. "What's she doing?"

"Are you sure it's a 'her'?" Ganesh laughed. "She's probably an Anarchist. There's a small society of them here who want to inject whimsy into Eidos. Even a little chaos. So they do strange things, like turn their body into a mermaid for an hour or two. You'll get used to such antics."

Will I? he thought. *Will I ever?*

A little later they came upon a debate in the middle of the avenue, with several hundred people gathered around. The aura of one of the women was an angry scarlet.

They stood at the edge of the crowd and listened. "Ah, there it is," said Aaji. "She's accusing that man of stealing her great grandson's position. She was his guardian, just as I was yours. She thinks he deserved the slot the other got. She's furious."

"Slot? What does that mean?" said Kiran.

"A rebirth slot. They both wanted the same mother, the same family."

"What? . . . My God, are there lawyers here!? Did the winner have a better lawyer or something? And who did the deciding? Or was there a lottery?"

Ganesh chuckled, then said, "A wise judge, or several, did the deciding. In the Bible there was a king named Solomon who had to choose between two women. Do you know the story? Both claimed the same child, and Solomon had to decide who the real mother was? If they couldn't agree, he would cut the baby in half, he told them. It was a ploy, but it brought to light the real mother. Because of that we call our judges 'Solomons.' Gandhi was a Solomon for the few years he was here. His business was assigning souls to their mothers. It's the most serious business we have in Eidos. And only the best men and women are chosen for the task. Not what you mean by 'lawyers' – though some of our Solomons were lawyers on earth. As was Gandhiji."

"Atoning for their sins, no doubt. God, this is a strange place! Are there many disputes over rebirth rights?"

"Plenty, and about other things too, but the light of the city soothes tempers. And most of us accept the rulings of our Solomons even when they hurt us. That woman was an exception. Nothing hurts so much as seeing our loved ones passed over."

"Where does all this deciding and judging go on?"

"In the Silo, up ahead."

Kiran studied the enormous dark structure and wondered if someday he would enter its halls. But then he rejected the idea.

"The Silo works closely with Records," Ganesh went on. "Histories are important. One's past life choices qualify one for this or that family. But so does kinship. You can imagine how much room for dispute there is."

"Incredible. And frightening."

"Yes. There are hundreds of courtrooms in the Silo, all buzzing with activity at the same time. And several thousand judges. There is what you might call a rebirth industry here, except that no one gets paid for services rendered! Disputes are common. But judgments are usually accepted in the end with grace."

"This certainly isn't any heaven, is it?"

"It depends. There are many happy souls here, souls preparing to move up to the next level. But you are right. There are disappointments and failures. Most Eidosians seek rebirth at one time or another, and there aren't that many ideal situations – by that I mean parents, families. Justice must be served, and justice often hurts in the short run. It can hurt intensely."

"Well, I for one don't intend to clutter the courtrooms with *my* little dilemmas!" said Kiran in a huff.

They turned toward the temple and began to walk again at a leisurely pace. They kept silence until Kiran burst out, "Rebirth! I hate the thought. Is there something wrong with me? Is it wrong to be attached to my mind and body just as they are? Should I be ashamed of this? Who knows what kind of body I'll have next time! Or even more scary, what kind of mind! Besides, how can I be said to be the same person I am now if I have a different body and brain? I know what you'll say: I have the same soul – "

" – and therefore the same character traits," Ganesh broke in. "And deep down in the subconscious even the same memories. That's because you've been the same consciousness throughout all your lives."

"Sick! Sick! You say, Ganesh, we can advance to a higher level? That's for me! I'm not taking any chances. That's what I'll do. Just show me the way!"

Neither Ganesh nor Aaji said a word more on the subject.

They reached the end of the avenue, which opened out onto a vast lawn surrounding the Temple. Thousands of people came and went, some in their native earth dress. These were usually visitors from other realms. Kiran spotted three women wearing headscarfs and asked Ganesh what they were doing in Eidos. They stood out.

"We'd have to ask. That's the costume worn by the women of Medina – Astral Medina. There's a lot of curiosity about rebirth, and Eidos gets plenty of inquiries from people living in realms that don't officially believe in it. Other visitors come just to experience the Temple."

The women passed by as Kiran studied them. They did not look back up at him.

"You said 'experience' the Temple, not 'see' it."

"Yes, I guess I did." Ganesh looked up at the great column of light reaching without end into a sky that was dark blue, what Eidosians called "spiritual blue."

"Do you feel its majesty, its compassion, its motherliness, its – its *divinity*?" asked Aaji.

Kiran stood still and tried to feel it. "No – I – I can't say I do. Not really. I'm afraid – I'm afraid I'm just a philistine. I was an atheist back on earth. Now I don't know what I am!" He laughed.

Aaji laughed too and said, "Your humility is becoming!"

They came up on the Hall of Records, and Kiran bent his neck back and looked straight up – just as he had when he was a boy and stood below the Empire State Building for the first time, two days after he got off the airplane from Bombay – so long ago. The sides of the building, stretching all the way to the top, were a fascinating collage of color – one of the afterworld's "Ten Wonders," and a favorite of astral tourists from other worlds.

"All those colors, thousands of them, in every design, are symbols," said Ganesh. "Not one of them is exactly the same as any other. They symbolize all the unique histories, millions of them, archived in the building – just as the single dark color of its sister building across the way symbolizes the common color of the womb. In Eidos, everywhere there is symbolism – symbolism and order. . . . Speaking of symbolism, get ready for some more. We're going to be going up, way up. Your file is based on your birthday back on earth."

"I don't get it."

"You'll see in a moment," said Aaji with a giggle. "Here, take my hand."

Up they went. As they glided past the sixtieth floor, Kiran noticed what looked like a layer of flowers holding up the rest of the building.

"What in the world? – "

"Oh, that's February 29, the sixtieth day of the year," said Ganesh. "It's one fourth the size of the other floors. It's there, but it's inset, surrounded by flora. Don't worry, the building won't topple over. Even if it did, no one would get hurt!"

"But why go to all the trouble? Couldn't they live with a little extra space on the sixtieth floor?"

"They could have," said Ganesh. "But whimsy can be fun. There's a lot of whimsy in Vimala if you look closely. Whimsy keeps the orderliness from becoming too predictable. Remember the mermaid?"

His birthday had been December 31. "Are we by any chance going to the top floor?" Kiran asked.

"Now how did you come to that, my boy?" Aaji teased. "Did you learn that in a logic class?"

They entered through a passageway emptying out into space along the building's side. His grandparents guided him through a maze of hallways and people until they reached a large room, a tastefully decorated clearing house. Bright, purposeful faces greeted him. "Another New Year's Eve baby!" sung out one of the women with a touch of irony in her voice. Yes, he was expected, and they were ready for him.

All beings who passed through Eidos since its earliest days over 2700 years ago were registered in the Hall of Records. From their memories earth's history could be recreated, even relived: country by country, neighborhood by neighborhood, individual by individual. It would be possible for Kiran to relive his great grandfather's tiger hunt with the local maharaja in 1898 or enjoy a leisurely walk through an uncongested Bombay in 1906. Hundreds of thousands of technicians worked in the Hall and served fellow souls in this way. Working with the Akashic Record – the record of everything remembered by every soul who had ever passed through Eidos over the last 600 years – they could bring to life the Boston Tea Party or Gandhi's Salt March or, for pure amusement, a memorable sleigh ride, all this with the help of unthinkably powerful computers using astral software – software that might someday reach back to Eidos's beginnings. They could even stage great historical theater, sometimes with the original actors if they were available. And the event would be staged as it really happened, not as earth's imperfect historians recorded it! Or, more humbly, the technicians could help souls like Kiran get in touch with their own past or an earlier past they had missed. That was their usual work, and Kiran took full advantage.

In the privacy of one of the Hall's rooms, Kiran entered into the history of his birthplace. He pushed back in time to the British period, then the Mughal, then the Portuguese. He watched the construction of the Colaba Causeway, rode one of the first trains between Bombay and Thane, and even sat in on the first session of the Indian National Congress in December 1885 – as it was experienced by one of its founders, Surendranath Banerjee. On and on the memories of bygone days and long-dead people came, and they diverted and fascinated him for a while.

But in the end he tired of all this history. Memories were important, but not other people's. What was important were his. What he needed was a complete playback of *his* life, all of it. This would be Judgment, with all its painful revelations.

Chapter 5

For a time Kiran lived more comfortably in Eidos. But comfort gradually turned into something a little like boredom as he tried to stave it off by reliving the past, traveling to other realms, going to concerts and dances and art exhibits, sitting at symposiums among philosophers, visiting museums, reading ancient astral palm manuscripts at one of the many libraries in Vimala, socializing with Aaji and Ganesh's many friends, and learning to meditate. At other times he threw himself into the games that Eidosians enjoyed, games that made chess or Scrabble or Bridge seem like child's play. He visited the wild animal park on Vimala's outskirts and roamed among the great astral beasts. He admired the replica of Yosemite and other earthly look-alikes. He attended a lecture by Charles Darwin: The great man, visiting Eidos from a more evolved sphere, gave a lecture on the Cambrian Explosion, in which he confessed to oversights he'd made in his famous book *The Origin of Species*, and Kiran joined in the conversation following the lecture. He swam in the superb crystalline water of inland lakes and enjoyed exotic birds and flowers. He sailed out in front of his house and lay on the thin sliver of beach next to the river. He attended the sacred festivals of light and music at the Temple and watched as the majestic sound produced by the orchestra molded the light overhead into an immense thought form of astonishing color and form which hovered over the orchestra. He even made a few friends and reminisced with them over earth. For a while his best friend was a South Indian girl named Uttara about Sonya's age whose career as a classical Koothu dancer had been wrecked by polio, which left one leg shorter than the other and eventually took her life. He watched her perfectly restored child's body perform in an operatic drama at the Hall of Dance. "But I want to go back to earth again where I can *really* be a dancer," she told him when it was over. Waiting didn't get any easier when Uttara gave him a final tearful hug before realizing her ambition. He missed her greatly, this little substitute for Sonya. Now there was almost no excuse to put off Judgment any longer.

When mulling over what Judgment must be like, he felt like a claustrophobic confronted with an elevator ride. He knew what he had to do, but he couldn't bring himself to do it. Aaji told him he would have to take the part of his victims. He would feel what they felt when he humiliated or rejected or bullied them. "It won't be pleasant, my boy," she had said. "You might run from it – you always have that choice – and that would be too bad. You should wait until you are strong, strong and determined." He thought of the two students whose worldviews he had helped mold and who later committed suicide. He thought of the women whose feelings he had trifled with and who had eaten their hearts out over him, especially Shalini. He thought of the colleagues whose careers he had manipulated and even ruined. No, he didn't feel strong and determined – not at all! He was ashamed of what he had done, profoundly ashamed, and that was good, Aaji told him. "But shame is not repentance. You've got to take it to the next level," she had said. No, he did not feel strong and determined. He was afraid. But he couldn't wait any longer. He would throw himself into the ordeal, come what may.

Chapter 6

H E pushed the door open and entered the Womb. . . . How
strange this place was. It looked like a large sensory-depriva-
tion chamber. Now he understood why Eidosians called it the
"Whale's Belly." There was no furniture except for a single chair, no
window, no obvious light source. Although it wasn't dark, he couldn't
see where the concave wall became the floor. He guessed the floor was
about thirty feet in diameter. The floor felt to his feet like suede, cool
and soft. The quality of the light was impossible to describe, for it had
no color. "Clear" is how he would describe it later. It was like the Light
of Eidos, yet it was different. It was alive, but it was unobtrusive. He
felt neither its love nor its judgment. He knew the priestess assigned
to him was nearby but couldn't see any trace of her.

Aaji had told him there was nothing he had to do. He ran his fingers
over the speckless, smooth concave surface of the wall, knowing that
it held great secrets that when understood would purge him and lead
him out of "the Desert." He didn't mind, not at all. Now that he had
taken the first step, he was stimulated. Now he felt really ready.

He sat down in the chair and waited as the room gradually darkened. He found this exciting at first, but by the time he was enveloped
in total darkness, he was apprehensive. He became aware of his alone-
ness, then remembered how close the priestess was. He began listening. He remembered a night back in California in the middle of the
Mojave Desert on a camping trip; it was so still, so quiet – not a breath
of wind, not a single cricket; the only thing he could hear was the hum
inside his head. Now he didn't hear even that.

Nothing happened, and he began to get impatient after a while, even to wonder if there had been a "mechanical failure" in the super-computer where his memories were stored. He was about to get up and prowl around just to do something, even start yelling, when the whole wall, its entire surface, exploded into white light and soundless moving figures.

He was electrified. It was as if his head was one giant eye; he could see every part of the concave wall at once; his vision was panoramic, he could see "in the round"; his vision had the same range as his hearing. Only the floor wasn't lit up.

The light that shone all round him and lit up the figures on the wall was identical to the living Light of Eidos, and he felt its strange, unde-terrable, almost menacing presence. The figures – they were mostly of himself! His whole earth life was passing by, panoramically, with incredible speed. But it wasn't exactly "passing." It simply was. It some-how displayed itself on the screen as a single ensemble, like a Table of Contents of one of his books. He didn't see only the things he had considered important milestones, such as his promotion to professor, but seemingly insignificant ones, like little Sonya's sitting on his lap as he patiently watched Mr. Rogers on television with her, or the contempt he displayed to a colleague who "confessed" he believed in UFOs – they were all there, the good and the bad.

Chapter 7

KIRAN had no idea how long he had been in the Whale's Belly. Time was irrelevant to his project; there was no deadline for completion. And time didn't govern the order of the playback either. Though he tended to move from more recent events to those more distant, he could move around as he pleased. He was like a coach analyzing the way a game was won or lost: Achievements or mistakes made near the end seemed more crucial than those made earlier, so he usually began the playback at the end and looked back. Death had been the logical starting place.

He found that events were clustered under headings – "files," as he thought of them. And he found it natural to move through one file at a time, carefully exploring it before moving to the next. There was a "Lisa file," a huge one. There were also files for each of his children and for each of his friends. There was a thick file for Shalini, very thick. Files could be organized in any way he pleased: by virtue or vice, for example. He began thinking of his life as a collection of files.

The Judgment moved slowly forward – like a caterpillar working its way across a pasture inch by inch. The Shelli Comer file stood out.

His relationship with Shelli began in 1983, when she was a student in the third class she took from him. This time it wasn't what he said in class, but out of class that did the damage. She was about thirty, was married to a decent man who bored her, had a son about ten, was suffocating in a religion she had intellectually outgrown, and was an excellent student. He knew from what she said in class she was exhilarated by the new sense of freedom he gave her. She decided to major in philosophy: She was the sort of student that made his job worthwhile, even delightful. He knew she was attracted to him as soon as she walked into his office the first time. Her eyes glistened, her face was slightly flushed, and her voice trembled a little. She had nice green eyes on a narrow face, a prominent nose somewhat too short, a determined jaw, a perfect figure, and an intense, hearty laugh. In a peculiar way he was attracted to her.

Shelli came to his office many times over the course of two years, and they became friends. He sincerely liked her, and in a rash moment six months into their friendship he speculated aloud what life would be like if they were ever to find themselves – somehow – married. They would travel often to India, he said; they would have a lifetime of exciting conversation, she said. They let their imaginations wander, and soon she revealed she was deeply in love with him and would do anything for him, including divorce her husband.

They sat in his office looking solemnly at each other for a few seconds after she made her confession. Now, lying in the Belly, he was inside her mind and felt her adoration and her pain. At the time it had pleased him to be so adored, and his face on the screen showed that pleasure. "What about your parents? How'd they feel?" he said.

"They would be hurt. They like Karl, and he likes them. But it doesn't matter. Kiran, I've never loved anyone like this before. Nothing else matters."

"Not even your child? What about little Matt? You would take him away from his father?"

"Yes, I would. My happiness figures somewhere in the equation, doesn't it?"

"Suppose I couldn't bring myself to divorce my wife. Would you be willing to be, well, my mistress?"

He felt her sharp disappointment, her humiliation, but her unwavering love as she said, "That would be better than what I have now."

Then she bowed her head into her hands and sobbed. "It's hopeless, I know!"

Underneath his gratification at seeing a woman caught in such slavish adoration was a very real compassion for her. He had wished he could give her everything she wanted, right there on the spot. He wished he could feel her physically dissolve into him; for he, like her, was starved for real affection. But he knew he couldn't. He knew he would have to let her go, and that the crazy game they were playing would have to end.

She was wearing a red sweater; an immaculate white lace collar neatly overlapped it at the neck. He stood up and reached out his hand, almost touching her on the breast. But at the last instant he let it fall awkwardly on the collar. He almost bent down and kissed her, but instead sat back down. He did not love her; he was not willing to break up his marriage and his home over her. Perhaps over someone else, but not her.

Kiran switched off the screen by concentrating his thoughts and willing it to stop – he had learned to do this – and sat back in his chair under the darkened dome. He loathed himself. "No, I didn't say that!" he said aloud in the dark. He wanted to fall at Shelli's knees and ask her to forgive him. But she was inaccessible, she was alive on earth.

The entire Shelli file unfolded in chronological order. He slogged through every significant conversation, every gesture, right up through their last time together on the eve of her move with her husband to St. Louis.

On one occasion midway through the friendship they had gone out for a cup of coffee; it was a winter evening, already dark though it was barely five. He told her to pull the car over. She was wearing a thick coat, possibly fur, but she shivered as she studied him in the gloom. Then he reached out for her and took her in his arms, squeezing her tightly. At one point he pulled back and looked into her eyes four inches away. He might have kissed her, but he didn't. Instead he hugged her some more, and felt he had done the right thing by not kissing her.

That hug changed her life in a way he didn't anticipate. A few weeks later she told him that since "that time in the car" the only way she could endure making love to Karl was by pretending he was Kiran. She said she carried the fantasy with her throughout the day and that it was the only thing, besides her son, that made life sweet anymore.

Toward the end he tired of her visits; he resented the time he gave her, for he knew the friendship could not deepen. He had work to do besides, and she was keeping him from it. His colleagues had begun to notice and to whisper. Mostly he simply found the too frequent visits tedious. But instead of breaking off with her, he chose to string her along. He could barely disguise his displeasure when she poked her bravely cheerful face through the door, but he lacked the courage to end the visits. Instead he took to teasing her. The screen played back the following conversation:

He asked: "How are things with Karl?"

"Oh, great!" she said with cheerful sarcasm.

"But he's such a good man, Shelli, and deserves so much more. Are you still fantasizing about me?"

"Of course."

"But why? If you'd married me when you were eighteen, how do you think we'd be getting along now?"

"Karl is boring, Kiran, that's all. And you're not."

"Maybe I'm worse things than boring."

"Like what?"

"Well, I'm critical, too critical. Did I ever tell you that you'd be a more attractive woman if you reigned in your laughter? It's shrill; it has a hysterical quality about it ..."

Sitting on his chair in the Whale's Belly, Kiran threw up his hands and shouted, "Oh, my God!" He switched off the screen with a vicious swipe of his will. "Forgive me, Shelli!" he kept yelling into the void as he paced in a circle around the Belly. He thought that what he said, indeed his whole demeanor, his strategy for "letting her down easy," was unforgivable. It was vicious and cowardly. If she withheld her forgiveness for all eternity, he couldn't blame her. He hated himself. He saw that the only reason for the friendship with Shelli in the first place was the kick that being so completely adored gave him; it made him, miserable man that he was, feel like a god. How he loved his power over her! What else did he love? Not much. The friendship was unnatural. For him it existed not because he delighted in her company, but to salve his battered ego. For half his life he had been recommending Kant's Principle of Dignity as the highest moral standard: "Never treat a person simply as a means to your own selfish gratification, but always as an end." It was the closest thing to a religion he had. But look how he forgot it when it made demands. What a miserable hypocrite he was! He used Shelli as an object, a plaything from the beginning. He demeaned her and turned her into a toy. Even his power over her was unnatural. What if he had been a fellow student in that fateful philosophy class instead of the all-wise teacher? Would she have adored him then? Not a chance. Not only was he a hypocrite; he despicably misused his office.

Long ago he had discovered he could stop the playback, "wind it back," and play it again while participating. He could mentally step into the script and undo his own mischief – not back on earth, of course, for what was done was done, but in the little world within the Whale's Belly under the guidance of the priestess. No less a perfectionist after death than before, he ran through certain episodes four or five times, as an artist standing before a canvas might paint his subject over and over until he's gotten it exactly right. These creative efforts demanded great concentration, for he had to guide not only his own performance but the performances of the other actors. This work brought him a certain melancholy satisfaction, for he felt a tender sympathy for his victims. And for Shelli he ended by feeling something very much like love. If only he could communicate it.

Chapter 8

SHELLI didn't provide Kiran his greatest lesson. This was reserved for Lisa. The following scene played itself out on the screen. The past once again became the present. He dived in.

The Philosophy Department had staged a debate on abortion, and Kiran, author of noted scholarly books on Camus, Wittgenstein, and, most recently, Derrida, had moderated. He thought the debate went well, and the large audience was responsive. He told himself that as chair of the department he should commend in writing his young colleague who put the panel together.

One of the panelists surprised him. She was the nun who defended the anti-abortion position, the Catholic stooge who was supposed to be the fall guy for the progressive voices of reason and enlightenment that would follow. Her non-dogmatic approach to the question and her nimble mind made him take note. But it wasn't just her mind that impressed him. There was something fresh and uncommonly genuine about her. She was not a walking filing cabinet of arcane information and argumentative strategies but a real person, a foil to all the windy buffoons who strutted themselves out as philosophers. She wore her ego so weightlessly that Kiran couldn't even find it. He remembered a quote from Chesterton, "Angels can fly because they take themselves so lightly," and applied it to her. "Sister Jackie" – that was the only way she was identified in the program. She laughed infectiously at herself when caught in a logical inconsistency, and she fielded questions from the audience with tact and compassion. The thing that impressed him most was something she said: "The choice to abort or not to abort must be informed not only by reason but, more importantly, by love." It wasn't the words that impressed him, but the way she delivered them. Her eyes incarnated the very love she spoke of; they transcended reason and argument. Kiran found himself wanting to agree with her even when he didn't.

Now, hours later, there was still a wonderful, almost visceral glow inside him. It was as if something brittle and thorny had broken up and been washed away, while something very ancient and all but dead, something left over from his boyhood in India, was revived and now flowed again. He wanted to talk to this woman, perhaps to share his life's story with her. He wanted to tell her that many years ago he considered marrying a woman he didn't love rather than asking her to abort what the two of them created. He bet Sister Jackie was driving back to Los Angeles that very night. Why not offer her a place to sleep? They could talk after dinner once the children and Lisa had gone upstairs. There was the extra bedroom, and the house was lovely. Sister Jackie would be delighted to be there.

His hand hesitated; then he picked up the phone to check with Lisa. He dreaded what might be coming.

"Lisa, I met somebody I'd like to get to know better. She's a nun, and I think you'd like her too. I don't even know if it's possible – she might have to go back to LA tonight. But if she can stay, I wonder if we could put her up."

There was a pause. "Well, I'd have to go out and get some things." Lisa sounded peevish. "I've been painting today, and the kitchen's a mess."

"She won't mind. She's a humble nun."

"To tell you the truth I just don't feel up to it. I'm tired, and I – I – "

Kiran felt his blood heating up. He knew when he picked up the phone this might be her reaction, but it always amazed him when he found it. He couldn't understand such inhospitableness, and it always infuriated him. It didn't really matter what he proposed. If it was short notice, if it took her just slightly by surprise, there was a fair chance her answer would be no. He would have to go for the compromise.

"Well, why don't I take her out to dinner, then bring her back?"

"We only have one bathroom upstairs. I'd have to get the bedroom ready and everything."

"*I'll* get the bedroom ready."

"I always end up doing the work – you know that. I just really don't want to do it, Kiran. If *you* want to do it, then go ahead," she said in that testy, persecuted voice that made him wince with hatred.

Kiran was tempted to bring Sister Jackie over anyway but decided against it. Though disappointed and angry, he gave in civilly. He consoled himself that probably nothing would come of the meeting anyway. People came and went in his life, and didn't he always remain pretty much the same?

The Kiran Kulkarni who at age forty-five drove home on a warm March evening from the California university where he taught philosophy epitomized the successful, attractive professor. Already he was in line for the vice-presidency of the American Philosophical Association, the first Indian ever to rise so high, and his classes were always among the first to fill. His classroom persona was aggressive, extroverted, and warm; it covered a sensitive interior that sometimes gave itself away by a nervous fluttering of the eyelashes. His personal outlook on life was fairly typical of an academic philosopher: Schooled in skepticism at Columbia, he tended toward atheism and stealthily steered his students away from religion.

If there was anything eccentric about Kiran's philosophy of life, it was his lately discovered attraction to India's mystical traditions, especially Buddhism, whose non-theistic mysticism blew soothing breezes over his over-exercised logical intellect. Kiran of course rejected "all that mumbo jumbo about rebirth" that was so dear to the Buddha and to the Hinduism of his family, but he longed for the transcendental peace of Buddhist meditation and sometimes wondered if he might study Buddhism after he retired from teaching.

On the political front he thought of himself as a fiscally conservative Democrat. He believed in balanced budgets, but not if they came out of the hide of the poor. Though not wealthy, he subscribed to *The Wall Street Journal* and knew how to make money in the stock market. He enjoyed watching his assets build, but he didn't forget his social responsibilities. He was not only sentimental about the poor but could get downright angry about their plight. Every month, over Lisa's protest, he wrote out checks to various Third World charities, mostly Indian. He was by nature thrifty, preferring to fix things rather than throw them away and buy replacements. That is how he came to be driving a seven-year-old white Toyota station wagon while Lisa, who rejected the logic of restraint, made her rounds in a sparkling new blue Volvo.

As a parent he tried to encourage in his two children a disciplined approach to life to offset what he took to be Lisa's impulsive, self-indulgent example. He loved his kids more than anything else in the world. Year after year he watched Ravi's soccer and baseball teams play their games, and he looked forward to following Sonya in volleyball and gymnastics. Though he was over-critical, he apologized at once when he was wrong. He was not much of a thanker, but he could forgive. Lisa had given him plenty of opportunity for that in their embattled marriage of nineteen years.

Kiran jammed his brains full of philosophy – or what passed for philosophy in the late twentieth century – in the evening hours before bed. Only in the last year did he permit himself a kinder form of recreation. He had begun to read novels, not as most people read them, but meticulously, painstakingly, penetratingly, with yellow marker in hand, as if every word counted. Now he was plodding through Marquez's *One Hundred Years of Solitude,* and he wondered why it was supposed to be *the* South American novel. The style was brilliant, but was that enough to make a novel great? He was half finished and determined to get through it; in the same spirit he swam laps in the University pool to keep his cholesterol down.

His mind drifted as he finally came to the end of another chapter. He thought back to Sister Jackie, and he was angry all over again. He might be sitting in the study downstairs at this very moment with her rather than reading about dirt-eaters in a depraved Colombian village. Lisa didn't even have to put in an appearance; and she would certainly not be bothered by the conversation, which was out of earshot of the bedroom where she was reading a novel by Ann Tyler. He really ought to say something. He ought to protest. On the way home he had thought of a way to make Lisa see how unfair she was being. He rehearsed the argument, then thought how he might best introduce the topic. He put the book, which had lain open in his lap, on the desk and closed it around the marker. He walked into their bedroom.

Lisa, as pretty at forty-two as she had been twenty years ago when he first met her, looked up at him in a daze as she lay back against the pillow in her nightgown with a sheet pulled up to the bottom of her breasts.

"Good book?"

"Unh hunh," she said, not looking up. "What do you want, KK?"

"Lisa, could we talk a minute?"

She looked up at him and let her hands holding the book fall wearily in her lap from the elbows outward, in the same way that a tree topples.

"What have I done wrong this time?".

"Nothing wrong. But I want you to understand how I feel about something," said Kiran, choosing his words carefully.

She stared at him with an expression of "here we go again!" and waited.

"Do you remember the time that Cathy asked if her boyfriend could stay over with us on the way up to Monterey?"

"Yes."

"Do you remember what I said?"

Then Lisa saw what was coming and flared up. "But Cathy is my *sister*. She's family!"

Feeling his temper rise, he controlled himself and asked, "What am I, Lisa? Am I not family? I live here."

"Look, I don't want to talk about it."

"But I do want to talk about it. I *need* to talk about it. Lisa, I don't think you've been fair." He waited for her to say something, but she didn't raise her eyes. "It wouldn't have occurred to me to deny my home to someone you wanted to bring in, or even someone your sister wanted to bring in. But you're telling me someone *I* want to bring in isn't welcome."

"I didn't say she couldn't come."

"Well, maybe not in those words. But you made it clear she wasn't welcome."

"You still could have asked her."

"Well, sure. But how would you have felt if I had? I have your feelings to consider, too."

"KK, you've always told me to say how I feel. That's what I did. I just didn't want her to come here *tonight!*"

"But tonight was the only time she *could* come. It was tonight or never."

"But you told me to say how I feel! That's what I did!"

"Lisa – Lisa – there are plenty of times I don't feel like keeping the children while you go out with your girlfriends, but do I make you feel guilty for going out?"

"But you're their father. Are you telling me you don't like being with them?"

"That's not the point! That's not the point, and you know it!"

"Please don't shout!"

Kiran was about to "lose it," and he had promised himself he would never let that happen again. Nevertheless, he closed the door to the bedroom so the children wouldn't wake up and returned to the battle, lowering his voice. "Lisa, I'm asking you to concede – to concede that there's a similarity between your sister's boyfriend staying over and Sister Jackie staying over. Do you admit this? Can you see that you're not playing fair with me?"

"No, I can't! You come in here trying to bully me with all your arguments. I can't argue with you! You are trained to argue! Now go away!"

"Lisa, you can argue fine. You don't like this *particular* argument because the truth is not on your side."

"The TRUTH! O-o-o-o-h, the TRUTH!"

The eyes of a wolf in frenzied attack could hardly have been less murderous than Lisa's. For an instant Kiran shrank back; then he steadied himself and said in a low growl:

"Lisa, I'm asking you to try to see what I'm saying. I can't live with a person who is so unfair."

"And I can't live with a person who is always *picking* at me!" she yelled.

Kiran stopped. Did he really mean what he was about to say, was itching to say? He thought of the kids asleep in their rooms.

"Lisa, listen to me."

"This is going nowhere! Please lea – ea – ve!" Her voice was that of an unwilling martyr confronted by her executioner.

He was not about to leave. He did not know what to say, but he was not going to leave. He was beside himself with rage, and every resolve he had ever made went out the window. "I should have married Shalini!" he blurted out stupidly.

"I – wish – you – had! You – de–served – each – other!" Lisa spoke each word with singled-out emphasis and utter contempt, eyes flashing hatred out of a face craning forward. "Or that Indian bitch your father picked out for you!" she spluttered.

He wanted to pounce on her and slap those hating eyes. But instead he said, "I'll be leaving by the end of the month."

"Then leave! Get out of here! Get out! Get out! You're a workaholic and a stingy bore!"

He shut the door to the bedroom and went into the guest bedroom where Sister Jackie would have stayed and sat on the bed in a daze. His head was pounding as if he heard a pile driver thudding in the distance.

He meant what he said. He did not say things he did not mean. He was leaving. He would get joint custody and make whatever sacrifice necessary to get out of his marriage to that appalling woman.

Suddenly he felt horror at the thought of breaking up his family and leaving the house he loved. He had to escape, to divert himself from thinking about this horror. He thought about his stocks. No consolation there – the market had been declining. He tried to think about the women he knew who might make him a better wife than Lisa and would be a good influence on Ravi and Sonya, especially Sonya, who was in danger of growing up as spoiled as her mother.

He thought of Angie Geeting. Wasn't she divorced? A fine mind, not pretty, but who cared? And Libby Dukes. She had even come on to him a little in the office. She could be exciting, he bet. No, Libby wouldn't do. Angie. Yes, Angie. Angie was a disciplined woman with a strong sense of identity. She was profound, centered, not diffuse and scattered and superficial like Lisa. Angie was the kind of woman he needed. A woman he could respect and admire. God, what it would be like to respect one's wife!

He thought of Shalini, dead so many years. It really was true that she would have made a better wife. The things that mattered to him then mattered little now. All he wanted was someone who would support him in his work, raise the children with good values, love him, and appreciate the love he returned. Who cared if she was a little mousy and neurotic? A companion, a person to sit by the fire with – she might be knitting while he worked on an outline for a new book or corrected papers. A person about whom he could write in his next book on the dedication page: "To X, without whose loving support this book could not have been written" – that's what he wanted, that's what he needed. That was the sort of woman he could love over a lifetime. He'd blown it when he married Lisa. Big time.

He realized he would never have such a wife and his feverish imaginings about Angie were sheer fantasy. He remembered Lisa's last facial expression, then thought of his own as it must appear now. He wondered if he, too, looked like a snarling wolf. His thoughts and feelings were grinding inside his head like crushed ball bearings that have lost their shape. Fire was burning in his chest – he knew that his hiatal hernia was kicking up, and he imagined stomach acid churning around at the bottom of his throat like hot engine oil. He wanted to curse and hit things. He thought of the Buddha with all his serenity. "Contact with the unpleasant" – that's how the Buddha described life. Again he saw Lisa's hating face and felt his heart contract and his breath grow shallow and hot. He thought of Sonya lying with her curls asleep in her bed, and the hatred simmered down.

What should he do? Like a broken-down destroyer being towed into port, he felt himself drawn to his children. He tiptoed into Ravi's room and turned on the closet light so he could see Ravi's face. There he lay, on his back, his breath going in and out in a soft purr. He was a handsome boy with perfect features; he might have been, should have been popular with his peers. Kiran felt the boy's private pain, his sullenness like a sharp lash on the back, for he knew where the pain came from. Should he have divorced Lisa years ago? But she would have gotten custody. So he had watched with growing alarm as Ravi hugged his hurt tighter and tighter to himself. "Don't you want to be out with your friends, Son?" Kiran would say. But on Saturday nights Ravi usually stayed home, studied in his room, listened to his music, wound himself all the more tightly in the cocoon of his insular world as his friends partied. Sometimes his heart almost broke for the boy.

He turned off the light and tiptoed out into the hall and into Sonya's room. There she was, her face in shadow. Again he turned on the closet light and looked at his sleeping angel. Suddenly he felt himself guided to his knees at the foot of her bed. He leaned on the bed with his elbows, covered his face with his hands, looked back up at her to make sure she was asleep. Then he let his head and upper body flop against the bed. Convulsions of sadness shook him. Not until Sonya, jostled by his sobbing, awoke and asked him in a child's pitiless, uncomprehending voice what he was doing did he get up and go into the guest room to sleep.

Chapter 9

O N earth he couldn't bring himself to admit he mistreated Lisa. But the huge "file" showed things in a different light. He witnessed her upbringing, the broken home she came from, the neglect and psychological abuse inflicted by her alcoholic mother, the fractured self-image and resulting superficiality, the futile quest for love and approval, the lies and self-delusions and vanities that protruded out of her troubled soul like submerged stumps. Why hadn't he seen this when they were living together? All this information was available if he had taken the time to look. Why didn't he? What was he doing instead that was more urgent? Studying stock charts? Writing still another paper to deliver at still another international meeting of philosophers?

After resisting the answer to these questions for a long time, the truth finally hit him. He had sacrificed all to pride and ambition – not only his marriage, but his passion for the truth wherever it might take him. Those Jesuits back at St. Xavier's had been right after all: Pride really was the original sin; and Lisa had fallen victim to his pride early. When she first stung him with her contemptuous tongue during the early months of their marriage, he was hurt to the quick, as anyone would be. But instead of overlooking these outbursts, which really didn't mean much, instead of putting them in perspective and shaking them off, in his pride and vanity he took them to heart and contemplated their heinousness. Instead of talking over the slight with her when she was in a better mood, instead of helping her confront her unfortunate habit or discover the real source of her rage, he clammed up and gave her the silent treatment, hardening his heart more and more as the months and years passed by. For a while he had tried confronting her, and the ungodly ruckuses that followed, like the one he relived, could be heard by the neighbors. And Lisa did not change. And he was certainly not about to change. So he went back to fighting in his calculating, logical way, and the arguments usually ended by reducing Lisa's position to absurdity, just as he might have in a philosophy colloquium, whereupon she would begin sobbing hysterically or shrieking like a small mammal in the claws of a great steely-eyed owl. In his bristly pride he refused to give her the things she needed most: forgiveness, compassionate guidance, love. All he took was sex, and little enough of that toward the end.

Off and on, as early as 1978, she suggested they go to a marriage counselor, but he always refused. As he watched these moments play back, they stood out in italics. Each proud refusal was a death-knell to the marriage. One humble admission that something might be wrong with *him* might have led to every kind of good, not only for them, not only for her, but for him too. When he first saw its truth, he jumped off the floor in amazement: It was at that exact moment that the buzz saw hit.

He had been more in the wrong than she! That is what the playback said, and that is what he knew now in his heart. All during the marriage he viewed himself as a long-suffering, heroically faithful husband yoked to a nasty, paranoid woman whom he stuck by out of some overgrown sense of duty that only a trained philosopher would be capable of, and because – there was no doubt about this – she was physically delicious and even at her worst served as a convenient outlet for his prurience in very unholy matrimony. But he more wrong than she? At the time it would have seemed preposterous. Not anymore. If only he could go back to earth and make it up to her. Oh what he would have given! But that wasn't possible. His work lay on his side of the great divide, not hers.

Then there was his ambition. If pride had undone his marriage, ambition had undone his ability to discover truth. As he watched the playback of his performances in national meetings of the American Philosophical Association, endowed lectures, TV debates, the many classes he taught, and informal discussions with colleagues and students all over the world, he was struck by how many times the truth stood right in front of him. Yet he seemed somehow to miss it. At first he could only marvel at this peculiar inability to see it, but as one episode after another paraded by, he became intrigued by his obtuseness. What caused it? How could he have believed, for example, that he was not a free agent (he called himself a "soft determinist")? How could he have defended this position in carefully worded papers read to international congresses and thereby denied the most fundamental truth of his nature?

Now he saw the whole truth, and it blasted him. On earth he thought his positions were arrived at through reason alone. And what could be more admirable than being reasonable? If one were wrong, which was always possible, even for him, that was of course unfortunate, but there was certainly nothing *morally* wrong about being wrong. Within the inner circles of philosophy he argued that no one could err morally anyway since no one was really free to do otherwise than one did. Before his death he would have argued for this position in front of God's very throne if God had existed, and on several occasions said as much. Now he saw it wasn't reason that had led him into error, but ambition. As a graduate student all he wanted was to be as esteemed and important as Leopold Kirkpatrick, his mentor at Columbia. Leo and Leo's colleagues taught him the philosophy that was in fashion. He mastered it better than any of the others, and his professors applauded. He was on his way. He began sending off his papers to the best philosophical journals, and three or four were accepted for publication when he was still in graduate school – an unheard of accomplishment. Then the job came, the exertion for tenure, the book that would secure the tenure. All had gone well, brilliantly well, and up the ladder he climbed, swiftly, way ahead of his junior colleagues, then even his senior.

In the race to the top, what had happened to the truth? He had been conned out of it by old Leo, conned in the same way Leo's mentor conned him a generation earlier. His search for the truth effectively ended in graduate school; his efforts since then had gone into shoring up the errors he learned there. New light? He had wanted no part of it. He was shown the time that wheezy old Digby – the department eccentric, stooge, and laughing stock, a believer in reincarnation and other metaphysical oddities – urged him to read a scholarly study on trance mediums and life after death. He had humored Digby, taken the book, kept it for a month, and returned it unopened. Now he realized that in that one ridiculous book there must have been fresh light. Perhaps there was more truth in it than in all the weighty monographs and scholarly articles that Leo threw at him put together.

How clear it was now! He hadn't taken the time to look for truth in the unfashionable places that the circle he ran with shunned. That, he now saw, was because he cared more for his own advancement in that circle than for the truth. Digby, that old fool he had ridiculed, Digby was a bold truth-seeker. And what was he, Kiran Kulkarni? A joiner. He could sniff out fresh grass for the herd, he might even lead the herd, but he had never broken away from the herd. He had a powerful intellect, but he had betrayed that intellect out of fear of the crazy places that truth might take him to. And truth was crazy, all right. It was so crazy, so surprising, so wonderfully unconventional that he found himself smiling, as if at a good joke. No matter that he had been the butt of the joke. It was funny all the same.

The Judgment went on and on in this damning, humiliating, yet oddly exhilarating way. First embarrassment, then shame, then remorse. Then genuine delight in the dawning truth. Finally an amazed incredulity that he could have missed something so utterly obvious. Always a dual process, a hybrid of incongruous feelings, a mulatto of good and bad, of penalty and reward. But none to accuse him, none to afflict him on the one hand or recompense him on the other – none, that is, except himself, the sternest judge of all.

Chapter 10

KIRAN opened a new file, the one he dreaded the most, the one that had caused him to postpone Judgment over and over until he was out of excuses. It was the Shalini file. She was the "other woman," the other woman who played so big a part in his life – or rather in whose life he played so big a part, a decisive part, a part he cared little to explore. But now the moment had come. He had no doubt he was in for another long, painful journey. But maybe this time more than self-knowledge would be expected. Shalini was on his side of the divide, and Aaji had told him she was in grave trouble and that someday he might be able to help.

Kiran opened the file.

There she was, just as he remembered her, as vivid as life. He watched her playing her cello. Did her father see something about her character when he bought it for her after she had lessons, when she was only eight years old? He could not have chosen a more appropriate instrument. Kiran saw himself asking her as they munched on a sandwich if she loved it more than him. No, she said, but then she added that the times she played the slow movement of Dvorak's *Concerto* were the most rapturous of her life.

Theology, literature, and the cello were lumped together into second place when Kiran made love to her the first time in his apartment. It would be an understatement to say that she adored him. She ate and drank and breathed him. She bathed in him and scented herself in him. She was aware of this, and she shuddered at the thought of what would happen if he should step out of her life. While doing research on Plath she came across a statement the poet made to a friend shortly after her husband left her, a statement she read aloud to him one evening: "When you give someone your whole heart and he doesn't want it, you cannot take it back. It's gone forever." At the time Shalini wondered if she, like Sylvia Plath, would someday have to climb that black mountain, that mountain of death, without a heart. Now he felt her fear.

She had always heard it was natural for a man's ardor to cool. Her mother told her it was a girl's greatest mistake to give all she had before marriage to her man. "And Indian girls would never even consider it!" she yelled. For the man would lose respect for her, and even if he didn't, he would have what he wanted. What reason would he have to marry her?

Shalini gave her all to him anyway, and his ardor, predictably, cooled. Yet everywhere else she looked, women were giving themselves to the men they loved without an eye to strategy. And obviously some of them got married. She decided her mother's advice was archaic and that it was simply natural for his sex drive to cool after two months. Yet a feeling of dread trickled through her when he didn't call or when they got together but didn't make love.

On one particular night she asked him if she could come over. It was the night before her presentation on Plath in one of her seminars, and she had the lecture down cold; she could have delivered it on a rumbling subway train or from a smelly barge on the East River. She hadn't seen him in three days, and now she wanted a break. At least that's what she told him when he resisted. The truth was she was almost sick with anxiety because he hadn't called the last two nights. He claimed he was tired but said she could come over.

She brought over groceries and put together a curry for him. It pleased her to see him relish it. But in bed as they lay holding each other he was somewhere else.

She called up her courage and finally asked what was wrong.

"Nothing."

"You can tell me, love. Trust me to understand." She was shivering.

"No, no, it's nothing." But he scowled.

"You know I have my lecture tomorrow morning."

"You'll do fine."

"I don't know. I've never taught a whole class before. And these are graduate students."

"You'll do fine, you know that."

Shalini could tell he wasn't even listening, and it both hurt and annoyed her. But she wouldn't show her anger; she tried never to show her anger in front of him; she had seen what that could do at home, where her father tyrannized over the whole family with his temper. "Have I done something to upset you?" she said.

"No! No, you haven't done anything to upset me!" he said in obvious distress.He jumped out of bed and went in to the bathroom.

Shalini shivered in the dark as she waited under the covers for him to come back. She wondered if she should leave.

He came back in his robe and turned on the light at the side of the bed.

"I'm sorry," he said. "It's just my faith. I mean, here I am studying theology and I'm not even sure there's a God anymore. It's insane. It's a charade."

She sat quietly and watched him.

"And I don't know about immortality anymore. I don't even know if there's a soul. Imagine what our family priest would think!"

She was enormously relieved she hadn't caused his distress, but his words nevertheless drove into her like dull nails. She knew he had his doubts, she even admired him for his rugged individualism. But there was a despair in these new words that frightened her. They smelled of something tragic, something defiant and sinister.

"But why, Kiran?" She propped herself up on her pillow and drew the covers around her body.

"Let's not go into it now," he said peevishly.

"No, darling, let's do. Please. Why have you lost your faith? All of us have our doubts, and most of us have revised our beliefs. I've begun to doubt many Catholic teachings – I've just assumed everyone has to do that, everyone who can think. And I don't know what to make of Christ. The deeper I get into Christology, the more I'm convinced that we're all walking on thin ice. So I come back to literature. It's my escape. It's real and solid, real people doing real things."

"How can you say that? Literature is fiction," he said with a trace of irony.

"Sylvia Plath's suicide was not fiction."

"Sylvia Plath. Always Sylvia Plath."

"Sorry. We were talking about you. Why have you lost your faith?" She pulled the cover, which had slipped down again, up around her breasts and looked at his dejected face as he swung it from side to side like a trapped animal. She was still shivering.

"It's the same old thing. The problem of evil. A God who's infinitely good and powerful, but who stands by and watches as children starve by the thousands every day. The thing that Dostoevsky saw in *The Brothers Karamazov.* 'So I give back my entrance ticket, and if I am an honest man I give it back as soon as possible.' Remember Ivan's words to Alyosha?"

"Yes." Shalini could hardly force herself to look at him. She was afraid of what he said, what he had become. There was something about him almost ugly.

"Well, that's it," he said sullenly.

She knew exactly how this argument against God went, and she knew how to counter it. But she didn't choose to now. "What will you do?" she said.

"I don't know," he said wearily. "Study philosophy I guess. Though frankly nothing is appealing."

These words stabbed at her, and now, as Kiran sat absorbed in the file, they stabbed at him. She wanted to ask, Not even me? Am I not appealing? But she was afraid to ask. She was afraid of what he would say. She thought of Sylvia Plath, of Plath's suicide. She thought of what some philosopher had called atheism: "just cursing." That's all life amounted to if atheism was true.

"Is that all that's wrong, Kiran?" she said.

"All? Isn't that enough?"

"There's a certain scorn in your voice. I lived with this. Dad talked to Mother that way all the time. Something is wrong, Kiran. Something is wrong with us, isn't it?" She could hardly believe she was speaking up this way, speaking so directly, confronting the problem head-on.

"Shalini," he said in a doomful voice with head shaking slowly from side to side and eyes blinking hard. "Shalini, I ..." Then he checked himself, closed his mouth, and nodded gravely, as if he had just realized some great secret or come to some final resolution.

"Kiran, what *is* it?"

"I'll tell you all about it next time we're together. There's nothing to worry about," he lied. "There's nothing to worry about."

"Here, darling, let me hold you," she said, holding her arms out.

He sat beside her on the bed and hung his arms around her. He seemed utterly spent. He was Sisyphus pushing his rock up the mountain, but without Sisyphus' spirit. "I'm very tired," he said.

She got dressed quickly, kissed him good night, and headed out. She rattled the door at the end of the hall and waited a second, waited for something, a mere "good luck." But it didn't come, and she left clutching his words, "There's nothing to worry about," to her breast. With all her might she tried to believe them.

Chapter 11

HE hadn't known what exactly happened on the day it all came crashing down on poor Shalini. All he knew was his part in it, the worst of it, the climax. Now he wanted to know what led up to it and what followed. He had to get into Shalini's mind and live that day for himself. He called out in his mind to the priestess to arrange it if possible – yes, he actually wanted to know. He was in a strange way enjoying Judgment. She said she could arrange it, but it would delay things. That was OK with him.

It was the day of her presentation on Plath. He joined in at the point where she put a series of painful questions to herself following the debacle. *How could it have happened?* she asked herself. *Wasn't I well prepared? Wasn't I the brain of the department, the student on whom all the professors pinned such high hope? Wasn't I destined to write scholarly articles at the rate of two or three a year? Wasn't I supposed to end up at Catholic U. or Notre Dame or Fordham, the first female head of a major theology department in the history of Catholic education in America? But I went all to pieces. Dan was clever, but no cleverer than future students would be.* She relived the dreadful exchange as she walked soundlessly along Fordham Road up the hill toward Riverdale. Yes, she would walk all the way home with her packed briefcase – four miles? She had a ticket to a play off-Broadway, she was supposed to go with Nancy. But how could she go to a play? So she gave the ticket to Nancy and told her to invite someone else. She thought of him, she wanted to be with him, to cry herself to sleep in his protective arms. But she would not let herself, she was not ready to tell him. What would he think? She would go home instead. She would go home to an empty house, for surely Lisa would be out. Yes, she would go home to an empty house and torture herself with the voice of Dan slicing and cutting her up into small pieces. She hated herself. She hated herself like those smashed roaches she was always flushing down the toilet.

It was stupid to be angry at Dan. He had been relentless, but he was always relentless, and she admired this trait in him. But she was angry anyway. She could not help feeling he betrayed her. She crossed the street over the subway and heard the "D" train rumble and screech underneath. Tears made her eyes blurry as she walked straight ahead in quick strides too long for her body. The road bent to the left, and the sun lay dead ahead just over the farthest buildings on the ridge. "I have suffered the atrocity of sunsets" – the words of Plath's poem descended on her and simmered in her brain. She could not have said how she got so far without being run over.

Dan had challenged her interpretation of Plath's motive for committing suicide. Shalini had thought this was her most original and exciting point; it was the climax of her presentation. She had made contact with one of the few Plath scholars, a man who had known Plath and felt that she didn't really intend to kill herself. He would be writing about this soon, and Shalini knew it would be hot stuff when it was published. It was with justifiable pride that she presented his theory to the class of graduate students at Fordham a year ahead of publication. It was a personal coup for her. The last thing she expected was trouble here.

"But it's irrelevant," Dan had said. They were sitting, a dozen of them, around a long table in Keating Hall. She was at the head, wearing makeup and a pretty mauve blouse – her "new look," as Kiran dubbed it. Father Haverstock – or "Dick," as everyone was calling him these days – was at the other end.

"She died, and she died by her own hand," Dan said in a matter-of-fact way. "You can speculate all you want about her motive, Shalini, but the fact remains that her late poetry is filled with death. It's everywhere."

Shalini was stunned. She couldn't see what he was driving at, but she couldn't see where he might have erred either.

Everyone eyed her, waiting.

"But – but – " She couldn't get anything else out. She swallowed hard and felt her cheeks burn. She lowered her eyes and shuffled through her notes, trying to collect her thoughts.

Dick tried to come to her rescue. "Dan, why doesn't it matter? If it could be established that Plath didn't intend to take her life, but was making a statement, or perhaps asking for help, then – wouldn't that be of interest to you?"

"Why should it be? Is that why we read her poetry? Do we read her *Ariel* poems with an eye to her suicide? Sure, there is death. But there is life, too. I don't want to be badgered into looking at her poetry through – through the monocle of her suicide. It would ruin it for me. She is too damned good! Her poems speak for themselves. Let them alone!"

Dick looked at Shalini: "What do you say to that?"

"Dickens was poor in his youth," she said. "Doesn't it help us understand *David Copperfield* to know that?" She looked beseechingly into Dan's menacing, almost ferocious dark eyes.

"It's kosher to look into an artist's *past* to understand his work," he retorted. "But you're looking into Plath's *future*. Plath hadn't killed herself yet when she wrote her *Ariel* poems. It's all speculation, Shalini."

"But there was the note to the babysitter telling her to call the doctor when she came in," Shalini said. "If the babysitter had not been locked out, Sylvia Plath might not be dead today."

"You miss my point," Dan said, squirming in his seat and throwing back his bearded head. "I'm saying that even if it *could* be established that she didn't intend to kill herself on February 11, 1963 – or if it could be established that she *did* intend to – it wouldn't be relevant. For she didn't write any poems *after* February 11!"

"But there is death everywhere in her poetry," said Shalini, "and that could be seen as prefiguring – " Shalini stopped mid-sentence.

Like a hot country lawyer, Dan saw her mistake and pounced. "I thought you were just now arguing *against* the thesis that she intended to kill herself. Now you seem to be arguing for it."

"No!" said Shalini, hoping that the word "No!" would be the abracadabra that called other words into being. But no other words came. There was an ungodly silence.

"Thank you, Shalini," Dick said at last. "Next class we'll look at the poetry of Ted Hughes, Sylvia Plath's husband."

That is how it ended, twenty minutes early. Now, as she whipped herself into a near-trot past the shops along Kingsbridge Road, new words out of Plath's poetry dug at her brain. "Out of the ash/ I rise with my red hair/ And I eat men like air." She had never had any feeling for these words before, but now she imagined she understood exactly what they meant.

When she reached the Major Deegan Expressway, she suddenly had an urge to jump off the overpass. Or rather a demon within her did.

Yes, a kind of demon, for she of course wanted to live. It was an absurd impulse, the sort of thing that might have occurred to her even on the best of days. It did not reflect a desire to die, not at all. Heights had always had this effect on her. They put the unthinkable in her head for no other reason but that death was close at hand. In truth death horrified her. She was the furthest thing from a Sylvia Plath. Perhaps she lacked Plath's courage. She would survive her humiliation and pull against the bit again. She could survive any humiliation. And she had him. Kiran! Oh, Kiran! He was too good to be true. What did he see in her? Would something take him away? The same feeling came over her as when she walked across the overpass. The loss of him was unthinkable, incalculable. Yes, he was too good to be true, but he was a fact. And in spite of all her fears, she had a presentiment that he would always be hers. He was her reward for a lifetime of humble service to others, of turning the other cheek, of dutiful living, of endless practice on her cello, of prayer. He was her reward, and God would not take him from her. Not ever.

By the time she reached Broadway it was twilight. She was beginning to look forward to getting home, still a half hour away. She loved the ancient hemlocks that towered above her little backyard apartment, her "bungalow," her "servants' quarter" behind her landlord's mansion, and she imagined the soft, whirring sound of the breeze blowing from across the Hudson through soft pine needles. It had been an extraordinary stroke of luck that she got such an apartment, even if it did come with Lisa. Kiran and she had talked about moving in together. They talked of summer evenings when they would walk down Palisades Avenue and look out over the water to New Jersey. It was a delicious thought, one that comforted her as she crossed the Henry Hudson Parkway in the dusk, no more than a mile from home.

She thought again of Dan. She saw his argument for the silly thing it was. How could she have been taken in? Why did she trust people when they said asinine things? Why did she take the trouble to look for the truth in what Dan said, when all he was doing was arguing to show off? Yes, that's all he was doing: showing off for Dick. Or perhaps there was a mean streak in him, perhaps he was a sadist who enjoyed scrambling people's brains. And that's all he accomplished. There wasn't the slightest merit in his point. Why shouldn't people look to the future to understand the past? Everything slid into the past eventually anyway, and Sylvia Plath's life was entirely a matter of the past. All of it was fair game for analysis. All of it fit together, all of it was of a piece. Dan's point was ridiculous. She wouldn't feel the sting so sharply now if she had lost out to a legitimate argument. But Dan had exposed her with his dirty trick as a fool. A dirty trick, nothing more, nothing less. Why did men use logic to bully women? Why did women *let* themselves be bullied by it? But what could they do when face to face with it? She had never found the key. She was always getting outmaneuvered; she could not think coolly enough; an intense emotional reaction would always befog her brain at the critical moment. Her battles were won only when the joust was over; she could keep up with any man on paper or in the private arena of her own thoughts. There she could expose every cheap shot for what it was. Now she felt only disgust, but whether more for Dan or for herself would have been difficult to say.

Fascinated, Kiran looked on at the replay. He dreaded what was about to follow.

As she passed Wave Hill now nestled in darkness, she thought of how tired she was. She concentrated on one step at a time, almost Zen-style. She felt her long, loping steps carry her body along up the incline. Perhaps she really did look like the roadrunner, as he once teased. In the first week of their love he admired the way she walked – he called it "unstudied" and "natural" – but twice in the last week he had been critical: he didn't quite say "unladylike," but she knew that's what he meant. How different, how graceful and beautiful was his gait – he was so straight and lean and masculine when he walked, yet so graceful. He reminded her of a general, or of Jay Gatsby decked out in a white tux on a summer night. She especially liked the way his knee snapped straight for a split-second at the farthest forward thrust of the leg, the way his hand flapped back smartly on the wrist when the arm reached its aftermost point, and the way his buttocks bounced up and down ever so slightly but did not move a hair's breadth from side to side. There was something almost jaunty about his gait, but it was accomplished with such fluidity of motion, such ease and evidence of good breeding, that the whole effect was magical. It was a unique blend of brahmin formality and lighthearted spontaneity. It matched the charm of his whole personality. It also excited her. She could almost imagine why men looked at girlie magazines.

Even more than her legs, her arms ached. She must have shifted the briefcase full of books from hand to hand twenty times. She thought of Gandhi's long march to the sea; this was hers. Finally she rounded the last corner. She opened the gate to the estate and found the flagstones with her tired feet. The apartment was lit up; that meant Lisa was home. Oh well, that was all right. Then she saw a car dimly silhouetted in the moonlight. That meant Lisa had company. "Shit!" she spat out into the dark in a most unladylike way, not at all like her. *Wait a minute. It's Kiran's car. What is he doing here?* Then she thought that Lisa must have borrowed his car, as happened once before. But no, there was music. Through the cracked window she heard Mozart, the *Clarinet Quintet*. Lisa didn't play Mozart; he was certainly there. Nancy must have called him and told him she had canceled out, told him something was wrong, and he had come over to surprise and comfort her. She remembered how his arms felt when they closed around her in bed. Greedily she dug the house key out of her purse and inserted it into the lock.

At this instant Kiran crawled out of Shalini's mind and stopped the playback. On earth suspense becomes unbearable when a critical outcome rides on the next moment. We hold our breath, dreading the worst at the same time we hope for the best. The possibility of loss, of failure, is unbearable. Kiran felt this way now, but not because he didn't know the outcome. He knew exactly what came next. What was unbearable was, he knew what would happen. Like an out-of-control skier headed for a tree, he reentered Shalini's mind.

She pushed the door open and caught a whiff of marijuana. "Kiran?" she whispered. But the living room was empty.

She listened through the music, her heart trotting. What was going on? No sound came from the kitchen. Then she heard Lisa's laugh. It came from Lisa's bedroom but was muffled. Shalini realized the door was shut, and her breath came fast and shallow. No, it could not be. It could not. She looked at the stereo; the Mozart was the last of several spinning records piled on top of each other. At that instant the second movement ended, and she took advantage of the silence to listen to sounds from behind the door. He was talking in a purr; he was saying something about his home, his family, his mother. All innocence. She would knock on the door. No, she wouldn't. But if anything was happening, she had to know. She tiptoed across the carpet to the door, her lungs barely agreeing to breathe. The next movement of the *Quintet* had begun, and she couldn't quite make out what he was saying. Another gale of laughter from Lisa. They were smoking, that was all. They were smoking in the bedroom because they knew she disapproved of pot and hated the smell. She held her breath, put her hand on the doorknob, then took it back. She would knock first. No, she would go outside and take a walk. But she was exhausted, and this was her apartment. She would sit down and wait. She would read.

Just as she made up her mind to tiptoe over to the sofa, the door opened.

"Shalini!" It was Kiran. His naked body shrunk back. The room was close with the smell of smoke and flesh.

Shalini gasped and stumbled backward. Out of the corner of her eye she saw Lisa yank the cover up around her bare breasts and look away.

"I – I thought you were – Oh my God!" He backed into the bedroom, covered his face with his hands, then jerked them down and, while on his knees, began feeling under the covers for something.

For Shalini it was Armageddon and Hiroshima all at once. Sirens screamed through her mind, spidery insects crawled across her field of vision. She hurried soundlessly out the front door. She did not feel the grass under her feet or hear the owl hooting in the cool, moonlit silence. She felt only a kind of black numbness. She was like a ghost making its nightly, mechanical walk at the scene of its murder a century before. Her mind was like an untuned TV screen with the volume turned up to a roar. Nothing of any specific content stood out; there was only the blast of white noise.

For Kiran it had been bad enough remembering what *he* felt at the time, but nothing like what he now felt inside Shalini's pain as he saw himself standing naked before her. Now he followed her movements outside the apartment. She forced herself to walk on, still bent over. Her breath rushed into her, and she sobbed hysterically. It seemed as if the next breath would never come, but she bent over as if to retch, and it did. She found the solid wooden bench next to the stone wall under the maple tree in the front corner of the yard, out of sight of the apartment. She sat down, pulled her feet up against her buttocks, put her arms around her legs. She was a little ball, no bigger than a brown nut.

For some reason she turned her head sideways and looked up at a few stray stars through the young new leaves. "Stars stuck all over, bright stupid confetti." Suddenly she hated Plath, but more lines swarmed at her out of the dark. "The heart shuts,/ The sea slides back,/ The mirrors are sheeted." Her mind hopscotched back into reality, and she heard the owl hoot for the first time. Six weeks ago they sat in each other's arms on this very bench and listened to that very owl. They had talk-ed about the children they would have. The boy would be like her, the girl like him. They would be brought up Catholic. She gasped, and a line out of C. S. Lewis drilled at her brain like an air hammer: "Real-ity, looked at steadily, is unbearable."

She saw headlights point up the driveway toward the road. Kiran. Kiran in his old blue Chevy, the "Mormal." It was so old and rusted out you could actually see the road roll by through a crack in the floor. She loved the Mormal, loved the things they had done in it. Oh Kiran! Kiran who had just had his first article accepted for publication in a major journal, Kiran on his way to the top ahead of the others. On his way . . . without her. Kiran who listened to her rhapsodize about Teilhard in excited whispers in the corner of the Library; she had seen tears in his eyes, just a few weeks ago. Kiran who took her out to deserted Jones Beach on a chilly April day and made love to her under a blanket as seagulls screeched in ecstasy. Kiran!

Suddenly she thought of Lisa and imagined herself clawing those blue eyes out of their sockets. She unwound out of her ball and sat up straight on the bench. She found herself feeling the tips of her nails, digging them into her flesh. She decided to go back into the house and confront Lisa. *Confront*, that's what people were always telling her to do. By God, this time she would! That's what Kiran would want her to do, that's what he would do himself. The thumb of both hands traveled sideways across the sharp tips of her nails as she walked to the house.

She got to the door and realized she didn't have a key. She picked up her hand to knock. She tapped faintly. She waited in the silence, listening for Lisa's footsteps, dreading them, hoping she wouldn't come. She picked up her hand and told it to knock hard, bang, hit, push the door in, confront the slut.

The hand froze, then dropped down. She slunk away into the darkness, slunk back to her bench, and rolled up into a fetal ball again. "Greasing the bodies of adulterers/ Like Hiroshima ash and eating in./ The sin. The sin." The lines out of Plath ate at the entrails of her desecrated literary brain. She felt like a turtle being batted about by a pack of jackals.

The screen turned black, and it was over. Kiran cowered under Shalini's hungry, desperate, pathetic love for him. He felt her insane grief, her self-loathing, her utter despair. He groaned under the weight of all this agony. He was appalled by his cavalier attitude as he dallied with Lisa and headed off to India on a vacation when so stark a tragedy was in the making. He had noticed hints of it and even written his best friend back home describing the situation, but what had he *done* about it? Very little. For the most part he had simply written her off and gotten it on with Lisa.

Chapter 12

Now the moment had come that he dreaded the most. He crawled once again into Shalini's soul.

Eight-thirty. A hot, sooty New York nightfall.

Shalini looked at the second hand of her watch as it subtracted what little time she had left. She had just put on the daring green mini dappled with tiny pink angels that they had picked out at Macy's a month ago – they had dubbed it the "sin sack." Today was her birthday, her twenty-third.

"Kiran, this is Shalini. How was your trip?"

Her voice had quivered when she called him earlier in the day, but he had answered airily. He said it had been fine. She didn't need to ask him when he got back – she knew almost to the hour. Every day, sometimes twice or three times, she walked by his apartment on Marion Avenue just to be near him, even though she knew he was in India visiting his family. To be near that apartment where he lived, where he bathed and shaved and dressed his precious body, both satisfied and stirred up her passion. She was like a researcher who misses a prized rat temporarily displaced from its maze. The rat will be back soon, its precious movements studied again – meanwhile there is the maze. Calling him every night and hearing his voice on the phone say its gentlemanly, accented hello had been her way of checking up on her rat before its removal. Now it was back; she had seen him on Thursday in the corner of the Fordham Library where he liked to study.

"Kiran, I was wondering if you had made your plans for the coming year."

For an instant she panicked when he said he wouldn't be back to Fordham, but then he said he would be going to Columbia to study philosophy. Columbia was a fifteen-minute subway ride away.

She tore off last month's page – June 1970 – from the calendar hanging on the wall and wrote in large red letters on the back: "Kiran, come in. The door is unlocked. I have business in the kitchen." She opened the entry door and stuck the message just below the peephole with scotch tape. A whiff of air lifted the paper, so she tore off another strip and anchored the note at the bottom. Then she turned on the outside light at the entrance.

"I was wondering how Lisa is." A nice way of beating around the bush.

She was fine, he said. She had sprained her ankle playing volleyball, but not badly. She barely walked with a limp now. Meanwhile she was taking summer school classes at NYU.

Shalini looked at the second hand steal by the six and begin another climb. She burped up something nasty. She hadn't been to the doctor, but she knew it was an ulcer.

She looked at the second hand climb toward the twelve, then glide by. *One – two – three – four,* she thought as it marched by the numerals one by one.

She looked around. Everything was in place – Sylvia Plath's *Ariel* poems open on the table to the poem titled "A Birthday Present." A birthday present, that's what she would give him. All wrapped up in his favorite pale-green mini. It would be splendid.

"I was wondering if by any chance you regained your faith while you were in India? Did you visit St. Xavier's and see Fr. Matthew?"

He hadn't answered her question directly. He said he found more beauty in his mother's flower garden in their backyard on Marine Drive in Bombay than in St. Thomas Cathedral.

"Then you are on the side of God," she said. "It takes God to make a flower."

"Does it? I'd say it takes the right sort of soil, temperature, and light."

Eight-thirty four. It was odd that no one from her family had called. Did they resent it because she didn't go home for her birthday? But why should she go home? Home to the father she loved but could never seem to please, and who might be drunk by the time she blew out the candles? *Oh Daddy, you see the mind I have, the mind I got from you, but why don't you ever tell me how good I am, that you're proud of me; and*

I was first cello in the symphony when I was still in high school! Home to her overwhelmed, unhappy mother who was constantly comparing her to her prettier, more outgoing older sister? *I'm not as pretty as Marcy, Mom, but I'm ten times as smart. Why doesn't that mean something to you?* She hadn't told anyone at Fordham about her birthday, not even Nancy, who would be moving in in a few days. No one except Kiran. And she had had to call *him*.

"I was wondering if by any chance you – you remembered it was my – birthday?"

He said he thought it better not to call. He said he thought it might make Lisa a little jealous.

Her heart had fluttered. If Lisa would be jealous, then Lisa must have seen he still cared. Was he tiring of Lisa? Was he coming around? A desperate hope – Eight-thirty five. No hope now.

"How – how is the Mormal?"

He had seemed surprised by the question. For an instant he acted as if he didn't know what she was talking about. Was it possible he'd forgotten the name from Chaucer she had given his rattletrap car, his "graduate school special"? She hadn't imagined that the lovable old blue Chevy could ever again be anything but "the Mormal," which meant an oozing sore. Had he rejected the name along with her?

Each of the questions she asked him she had written on a piece of paper, just to make sure she didn't forget anything. Now she came to the one thing she needed to tell him. It was horrible that it came up so soon, but she couldn't think of any way to put it off. She froze as she studied the question, her belly knotted.

"Kiran?"

"Shalini, is there something you want? Can you come to the point?"

"Kiran – Kiran, I'm, I'm pregnant."

"You're *what*?"

"I don't know what to do."

"*Baap re!* Oh my God! By whom?"

She was shocked. "By, by *you*, of course!" She felt like screaming at him, screaming every filthy thing she had ever heard men say to each other.

"Goddamn!"

"I'm sorry."

"How could you have let this happen? I thought . . ."

There was a pause. She imagined him writhing in his seat holding the phone. She waited.

"What are you going to do about it?"

She hadn't planned on saying it. She had thought about it, but she hadn't planned it. Actually she had quite specifically rejected it. But she said it anyway. "Kill myself."

"Well go ahead and do it! That would solve all our problems!"

"I'd like to see you first."

"Shalini, I'm sorry. I didn't mean that."

"Is Lisa there?"

"No."

"Kiran, if only you knew what a pure, loving heart mine is."

"Shalini –"

"Kiran, I've seen you love me back. I've seen your happiness when we were together. I haven't changed. You haven't changed. We can have that again. Why can't we have that again? *Why*, Kiran, *why?*"

"Shalini, Shalini – " He was confused.

"Kiran, do you remember the time in the Library when I was telling you about Teilhard de Chardin? There were tears in your eyes. Do you think you can have that with Lisa? And the time at Jones Beach wrapped in the blanket with the seagulls screeching overhead, as if in ecstasy, and on the bench under the tree here at the bungalow? And the plans we made as we looked out over the Hudson? And – and the birthday present you said you would give me? It was a ring, wasn't it? Today is my birthday, Kiran!"

There was silence at the other end of the line, and Shalini let her heart hope that he was coming to his senses.

"Shalini, we have been over all this before. Lisa –"

"But do you think for a moment she loves you like I do? And she lacks my intellect. You'll tire of her, Kiran. Do you really think for a moment she could make you as happy as I could *in the long run?* Do you–?"

"Yes. Yes I do, I'm afraid. That is exactly what I think. And more so. I'm sorry."

She had begun to shiver all over, she could hardly continue the conversation. "Kiran, I really want to see you tonight," she said in a wobbly, whimpering voice. "Tonight is my birthday. And you promised."

"Shalini, I can't come, you know that."

"At nine o'clock. I will be here in the bungalow."

"Shalini . . . no."

She hated herself for what she said next, but she couldn't help it: "Then I, and your child, will be dead tomorrow."

"No! Shalini! No!" He was beginning to panic, and a savage instinct deep down in her was glad. But everything else about her loathed the thing she was doing.

"Nine o'clock, Kiran." She felt split in two. She felt that some kind of demon inside her spoke these words. With all her might she despised the demon, yet she didn't contradict it. She was like a man playing "chicken" with his car as another is rushing at him sixty miles an hour. She would not turn away. She would not turn away even if it killed her.

He was calmer. "Shalini, this is blackmail. Blackmail, yes. And you say you love me so purely. All right, maybe I'll be there. Maybe we'll come up with something. Shalini, but what you are doing is contemptible. Don't you know that? It's contemptible, unforgivable."

Eight-forty. The air was stagnant and hot. There was a window air conditioner in the living room, but she used it only when Nancy wanted it on. And Nancy was vacationing with her family. It was twilight outside, pinkish and grimy. No one had said happy birthday. No one seemed to care whether she was dead or alive. Not even God, for wasn't he dead, just as the theologians were saying? Why go on living? She had lost her scholarship, she had been demoted to a grad assistant. She had almost lost her faith. She got rattled when she tried to teach. She had an ulcer. She hadn't touched her cello in two weeks. She was carrying his child, and that might have been something to live for. But he didn't want it.

One – two – three – four, she thought as she watched eight forty-one decompose.

It was time. With the same sense of playing "chicken" she felt on the phone, she shut the kitchen window. She opened the oven door of the stove and blew out the pilot light. She picked up the lid and blew out the pilot lights under each of the four burners.

Eight forty-two. She would probably be unconscious when he walked through the door at nine o'clock. What if he was late? He was always prompt, but what if? And what if he didn't come? He only said "maybe." But that was the chance she would have to take. She didn't care anyway. What was there to live for if he didn't come?

She had written out the telephone numbers of the ambulance company and her doctor. She had written them out in large red numbers. Everything was set. The note sat neatly open on the kitchen table where he could not miss it. She was wearing the dress he picked out for her.

She closed the kitchen door and went to the stove. She reached down to the oven dial and turned it clockwise as far as it would go. Then, using both hands, she turned the four dials for the stove to the full "on" position. She felt a certain thrill as she did the deed. But she also felt it was not really she who was doing it, but someone else inside her.

She could smell the gas jetting out into the kitchen.

Eight forty-five. She sat down at the table and faced the stove. In front of her on the table was Sylvia Plath's poetry from the last months of her life. It was opened to "The Birthday Present." She thought of Plath, communed with her, couldn't help feeling Plath was there with her in the room. Plath had done it with gas too, done it over a man, only seven years ago. Shalini thought of herself as a "second Sylvia" re-enacting the deed that cost the "first Sylvia" her life. Except that, of course, he might arrive in time to rescue her. Would she still be warm when he got to her? Or perhaps he might be early. She decided to pretend to be unconscious if that happened. No, that would be a lie.

The gas swelled through the kitchen, and her head began to throb slightly. "Sweetly, sweetly I breathe in,/ Filling my veins with invisibles, with the million/ Probable motes that tick the years off my life," she read.

A part of her was horrified at what she was doing. How could she even pretend she deserved him after this? He would despise her forever, and she would deserve to be despised. But then she remembered he had already learned to despise her, and for no good reason. For no reason at all. She would make him pay dearly. He would see what he had done.

Eight fifty. She was beginning to feel woozy. She looked down at the book and her eyes fell on the line, "There is this one thing I want today, and only you can give it to me."

Suddenly she thought of the baby in her stomach. For an instant she was overwhelmed by guilt. What if she should die and the baby went with her? It would be his fault. If he didn't come, if he wasn't on time, it would be all his fault. What if the baby did die? He didn't want it anyway.

She looked up at the oven with its door yawning open. Inside she saw – what exactly was it? – a huge turkey, yes, a living turkey with mean, gleaming eyes. Somehow she knew the turkey was sitting on a golden egg, and that that egg belonged to her. She wanted the egg, but the turkey was guarding it. She would not be able to get beyond the door before it began viciously pecking her. She stared at the door long and hard and was frightened.

As if remembering something from another world, she looked down at the watch. Eight fifty-six. She thought she might want to stop what she was doing, but she did not budge. She had written she had business in the kitchen, and wasn't she a woman of her word? She looked down at the poetry book but turned away in disgust. What if she died and God was waiting? God. How would she meet him? She would give him her baby, the baby she was killing, as a sacrifice. Abraham and Isaac. She would put her baby on the altar of God. God would accept her then. God would understand.

She looked over at the oven door. There was the turkey staring at her. It sat on the egg, her birthday present. The turkey looked like Kiran. Yes, it had his face, it *was* Kiran. And he wouldn't give her her birthday present.

She put her head down on the table as if to weep, for she felt very sad, very, very sad, and so alone. Slumped against the table, she felt the whole world resting on her, but ever so softly. It made her sad, but did not crush her. It did not make her cry. No, she did not wish to cry. In fact there was something almost pleasant about being able to rest her head on the table. She did not know why she was feeling almost happy, so restful and sleepy. Yes, she just wanted to sleep. She forgot all about the turkey in the oven, all about him, all about God. A warm but heavy fog settled over her as the first stars twinkled outside the window. At 9:05 he called her on the phone, but she didn't answer.

Chapter 13

KIRAN knew he would have to follow Shalini into the Shadows following her death. Only in that way could he feel the full shock of what he had set in motion. Only in that way would the Judgment be complete. But he could not face the full truth, not yet. Watching the suicide unfold, feeling Shalini's anguish as his own, but feeling it without the anesthetic effect of flesh, feeling it in its unbuffered horror, as if multiplied by a factor of three or four, feeling it in his astral brain as a hammering, stabbing pulsation – no, he could not take the final step. Not yet. He would step outside of her pain, see it from a distance, see it through the eyes of a third party. Yes, there was a conversation. He would relive that. It wouldn't be off-topic, but it would be bearable. It might be beating around the bush, but that was allowed.

A man of about sixty, Dr. Leopold Kirkpatrick was a highly respected eccentric who taught philosophy at Columbia University in New York and had written several books in the analytic style. At the Low Memorial Library he was once arrested for hitting golf balls with a four iron along the length of the portico supported by its ten fluted Ionic columns. According to one account, the preferred, he was trying to demonstrate by his bizarre activity the freedom of the will, while according to another he was merely taking extreme measures to cure a slice. Another time he flew a kite from the raised arm of *"Alma Mater,"* the larger-than-life bronze statue in front of the Library. On one side of the streamer which served as the kite's tail he painted in Latin the motto of the University, *"In lumine tuo videbimus lumen,"* while on the other he painted the translation, "In thy light shall we see light." Ever the teacher was Leopold Kirkpatrick.

It was Dr. Kirkpatrick who happened to be in the philosophy office when Kiran walked in to ask about graduate work in philosophy.

"Fordham?" he growled as he overheard Kiran tell the secretary where he was studying. "Are you a Catholic?"

"Sort of," Kiran said as he turned toward a face with leathery red jowls over a yellow necktie loose at the collar.

"And did I overhear you tell the secretary you scored a 1520 on the GRE?"

"Yes. But that was a few years ago. I was in a seminary for three years."

"You were studying to be a priest, eh? Doesn't matter. Those your transcripts?"

That is how they met two months before, and Dr. Kirkpatrick had gone out of his way to see that Kiran was accepted quickly into the philosophy program. At one point during that first interview he asked Kiran how he liked the Jesuits.

"Oh, they come in many stripes."

"Hmmmm." Kirkpatrick looked up with eyes that made Kiran feel like a butterfly being pinned to its mount. "We'll unpoison you," he said with a quick, wicked grin.

Kiran felt exhilarated by that first meeting. He sensed that Kirkpatrick for some reason had taken a shine to him – "Call me Leo," he said near the end of the interview – and Kiran for his part liked the earthy man who picked at his nose behind his desk, told him there was a great adventure in store, and gave him his first piece of philosophical advice.

"You haven't read Wittgenstein's *Tractatus?*" Leo asked gruffly but with a teasing twinkle in his eye.

Kiran had gone out and bought the *Tractatus* straightaway.

"Who?" Leo blurted over the phone.

"Kiran Kulkarni, the fellow from Fordham, the fellow you wanted to rescue from the Jesuits."

"Kiran, of course, how *are* you?" Leo was all amiability.

They had made arrangements to meet under the portico of the Library, the same that Leo had immortalized with his four iron. Two months had passed since their first meeting.

The heat that had gripped New York for the better part of a week had broken overnight, and a delightful breeze blew in across the Hudson as they crossed the Upper Quadrangle and then turned down College Walk toward Broadway. Though late August, it was almost sweater weather.

They passed between rows of trees through the great iron gates, crossed Broadway, and turned north. Inside the Barnard College courtyard on their left, young men in scruffy beards and long, unkempt hair lay next to formidable bra-less females in granny glasses and faded blue jeans. Army knapsacks with peace symbols sewn on decorated the bright grass. Leo was chafing over some colleague of his he disliked. "A man of high principle and no interest," he concluded with a confidential chuckle.

As they walked along at a brisk pace, Kiran wondered if he had come to the right man after all.

"What's on your mind?" Leo said abruptly. "Second thoughts?"

"No, not at all," said Kiran, hopeful that they would get down to business at last.

"You're Indian, aren't you? But you're not a Hindu or a Muslim? But a Catholic?"

"Actually I am Hindu, but I went to a Catholic school in Bombay and, uh, converted."

"Was that a problem for your family?"

"Oh, God, yes!"

"But it's not a problem now, so what can I do for you?"

"It's – uh – I just didn't know who to go to."

"Are you a homosexual?"

"Oh, no."

Leo slowed his pace and patted Kiran on the back. "Wouldn't faze me a bit if you were, you know."

They walked twenty more steps in silence as traffic rushed by. "It's just that . . ."

"Go on," said Leo with a hint of impatience in his voice.

"A girl killed herself over me."

The swish of the trees in the wind overhead accentuated the silence that dropped between them. Their pace slowed perceptibly. The traffic seemed to crawl by.

"Why did you come to me with this? I'm not a counselor," said Leo.

"I don't need a counselor. I wanted to know what you made of it. I know what the Jesuits would say. The immortal soul is released and goes to judgment. I read Wittgenstein like you told me to, and – uh – I respect you. But if you'd rather not go into it . . ."

"Not at all, not at all!" said Leo, waving aside Kiran's hesitation. "We'll go into it. But first tell me what *you* think."

They turned left on W. 120th Street and headed toward Riverside Church, with its massive Gothic spire reaching up toward God in the bright afternoon sky.

"I hate to think," said Kiran, "that all this talk about an immortal soul could be a delusion, a delusion for the faint of heart. I'm afraid I'm one of the fainthearted myself."

"What makes you think that?" said Leo cautiously as they turned right on Claremont and walked in the shadow of the great church. "But first tell me, did you love the girl?"

"I thought I did. But no. I cared, I guess. Yeah, I cared. I cared a lot. And it was such a great waste."

"What was her name?"

"Shalini. She was gifted. Very gifted. But fragile. She loved words. She played with words, enjoyed words. She would turn them inside out, speak them spelled backwards, reverse their syllables, do all kinds of crazy things with them, and expect me to understand. She played with them like toys. It was fun. And she loved the cello. And, and what a fit."

"Fit? What do you mean?"

"Well, the cello's pitch fit her personality. You know how a violin sounds. Its high pitch was too – too ecstatic, too vibrant for her, and the heavy tones of the double bass were, well, too masculine. The cello was exactly right. Its high notes are, well, muffled, and its low ones are like – these were her exact words – 'like the groans of a dying man.' The cello 'mingles beauty with death,' she said another time. She could have gone to Juilliard and played in a symphony orchestra or something. She sometimes second-guessed herself for not doing so. But she loved literature, loved words, even more than music, and close behind that was religion. So she went to Fordham instead. She had a full scholarship in the Theology and Literature program of the Graduate School. The only one they gave that year."

"And you jilted her."

"I – I did."

"And you're consumed with guilt."

Kiran considered for a moment. "Profoundly. I remind myself that people fall in and out of love all the time. We weren't married. I hadn't made any vow. But guilt? Oh, yes."

"Were you by any chance the first boy she made love to?"

"We were both virgins."

"She was the first girl you planked?!" Leo asked in surprise.

Kiran felt blood rush to his face. It irked him to hear an act he thought of as sacred spoken of in such a way. He considered carefully what to say. "I don't know that word, but I think I know what you mean. Yes, she was. In India we are very careful about – giving ourselves before marriage. You could describe us as puritanical."

"I can be pretty crass," said Leo. "Where were we?"

"My girlfriend – we're pretty serious – I'm angry at her. If I hadn't listened to her, Shalini would be alive right now. You see, she didn't really want to kill herself. She was making a statement. We had arranged for me to meet her at a certain time, and she expected me to find her unconscious but not dead. But I was late. I'm *never* late. But this time I was. Her body was still warm, but she was gone. It was pretty horrible. I tried to breathe life back into her, so did the medics, but we were too late. Just a mass of flesh. And she was carrying our child."

"Child? How far along?"

"Six weeks, maybe. She had just found out."

"How do you feel about that?"

"Not exactly guilt. Sadness, deep sadness. But I remind myself what a mess it would be if that child had come into the world. That's the last thing I needed."

"You're right about that. Though some of my students somehow manage."

They took a left on West 122nd Street, and there was the Hudson River spread out in front of them and gleaming in sunlight. Kiran remembered the times he and Shalini had walked along the same river a few miles upstream. The servant's quarter they called "the bungalow" in the backyard of an estate, their plans to move into it together, the ring he had planned to give her on her birthday, the good Catholic children they, or rather she, would raise – he suddenly felt like sobbing, then cursing. It was a sorry world. A sorry world in an indifferent universe. A world devoid of meaning. He remembered Camus' famous phrase "the benign indifference of the universe." When he first read it six months ago, he found it magnificent. But there was nothing magnificent about it now. Benign? Who was Camus kidding? There was nothing benign about Shalini's death, as the funeral in Port Washington made clear. Her death was a stark tragedy. The priest, to his credit, did not dance around this fact. His short sermon, discharged with feeling to a benumbed, wet-eyed gathering of students, family, and family friends, hit home.

"It's not clear to me why you're angry at your girl friend," said Leo as they crossed Riverside Drive.

"She persuaded me – they were roommates, opposites, rivals – Lisa, that's her name, was furious at Shalini when I told her where I was going. You see, Shalini blackmailed me into coming over to her apartment; it was her birthday; she threatened to kill herself if I didn't come. Lisa got upset over this. 'At least be late!' she yelled. She was jealous of Shalini, afraid I would go back to her. 'Don't give her what she wants, at least be late!' she kept saying. I told myself it wouldn't hurt if I were a half hour late, as long as I finally got there. So I caved in. But that half hour was the difference between life and death. She did it with gas. Everything was precisely timed – she was always a perfectionist in everything she did. I'm sure she expected me to get there in time to save her. And I would have if I hadn't been late."

They had come up on Grant's Tomb. A few Japanese were snapping pictures. Perhaps they hadn't heard the venerable site was no longer a choice tourist attraction, but merely the northern terminus of an eccentric Columbia professor's daily constitutional.

They paused at the bottom step of the monument and gazed up at it. "I'm sorry, my boy," Leo said as he lightly patted Kiran once on the back. "By the way, was there any chance your girlfriend was right?"

"About what?"

"About going back to Shalini."

"I probably would have if she had decided to have our child. I would have had to. I had disgraced myself and the family when I converted to Catholicism years ago. I couldn't make a mistake that grave again. I would have married a girl I didn't love and rejected the girl I did love. I would have raised that child with Shalini and made the best of it. It might have been hell, but I would have done it."

"And now there's nothing preventing you from marrying the girl you love. How do you feel about *that*?"

Kiran shook his head slowly. A faintly ironic smile twitched at the corners of his mouth. "There is one thing I'm not exactly proud of," he said. "I'm really embarrassed to tell you this, but I'm going to anyway. Yeah, this has been bothering me. When I knew Shalini was dead, mixed in with all the grief and confusion was a – God I hate to admit this! – a kind of elation, real joy." He looked straight at Leo. "Can you imagine that? Joy!"

"Go on."

Kiran swept his head from one side to the other in a quick, wide arc as if trying to free his mind from so terrible a memory. "This is the great irony," he went on. "By taking her life Shalini relinquished all claims to me. I was free. Do you know how low I feel when I remember that feeling of joy? Joy! My God!"

"Wait a minute now," said Leo. "Anybody could have felt what you felt. I sure as hell would have! But few would have had the lucidity to see it. You can't control what you feel anyway, only what you do. You're a philosopher, and I expect more of you. Philosophers are not hemmed in by convention. Society says you should feel grief, grief and nothing more, in a situation like yours. And you've bought into its values. Leave it behind. If you felt joy, you felt it. You didn't flaunt it, you just felt it. There is nothing dishonorable in feeling it."

Kiran looked at Leo and marveled. He wanted to hug the man. Leo had understood. The way Leo explained it was exactly the way he had explained it to himself a hundred times. He just hadn't expected anyone else to understand. So he put himself through the stupid ritual of shame to fence himself off from Leo's condemnation. But, instead, Leo had understood! He loved Leo. A bond of almost childlike trust formed in his soul.

Kiran looked up at the monument. "Grant's Tomb. Who was Grant?"

"He's the man who's buried here," said Leo with a chortle. "Just an insignificant general who fought on the wrong side of the Civil War. I'm from the South."

Kiran didn't understand. "I was pretty good in science and languages at St. Xavier's," he said, "that's in Bombay, my hometown, but not so good in history." Then he looked at his new mentor in wonder. "Thanks," he finally said. "Thanks a lot."

They walked up the steps into the interior.

"I don't care for the mosaics," said Leo. "See up there over the windows? There is Grant's victory at Vicksburg, over there is Chattanooga, and there is Lee's surrender at Appomattox. Not the stuff a Georgia boy like me much likes."

Kiran looked up at first one scene, then the other opposite, then the third.

"But of course I'm only being facetious. All the principals in that story are dead now anyway," Leo continued, "so it really *doesn't* matter, does it?"

Kiran had forgotten the original reason for seeking Leo out, but now he remembered. "Just how dead *are* they, do you think?"

"Hmmm." Again there was a twinkle in Leo's eye. "How shall I answer that one?" Leo guffawed out a "huh!" then seemed to compose himself for a lecture. "Before I tell you what I think, let me tell you what a colleague of mine would say. Let's call him Professor Pollyanna. Actually he's not a bad fellow. And since he's not in philosophy, he's harmless enough. Now Professor Pollyanna has done a lot of reading in psychical research. He reads transcripts of mediums. It's a kind of hobby of his. He believes –"

"Excuse me, but I don't know that word. What is a medium?"

"That's odd. I thought India would be swarming with them. A medium is someone that spirits talk through. You know, dead people. That kind of spirit." He chuckled, then went on. "So what would he say about your girlfriend? Well, he would be absolutely sure she was alive. What she was experiencing over there – well, that would depend on who she was here. You say she killed herself. That might mean trouble for her, big trouble. She could be stuck somewhere, stuck in her own dream world, living in her dreams as if they were reality. And since she killed herself and now feels guilty, they might not be very pleasant. Do you get the picture?"

"I think so. Rural Indians believe in that sort of thing."

"Or she might be lurking around the scene of the crime. Or around you, for that matter, heh heh! It would depend on her expectations and drives. These would create her fantasy world. You might be wondering where God fits in. Pollyanna says that God has nothing to do with it. God doesn't judge her; she judges herself."

"And you don't agree with this?"

Leo chuckled. "It doesn't matter whether you're buried under a humble grave marker in a cemetery in Port Washington, like – what's her name?"

"Shalini."

"Or in a sarcophagus of polished red granite, like Grant and his wife below us. It all comes to the same thing."

"So you don't believe in the soul."

"The only souls we have are on the bottom of our shoes," said Leo with a glorious smile as he held out his hands like a diva hitting high C. "Get over the guilt, the regret, whatever it is, my boy! There is no one who'll punish you except yourself. What's done is done. If you made a mistake, learn from it, but don't fret about it anymore. This is the only life you'll ever live. 'A flash of light between two eternities of darkness,' said a wise man. Make that flash *flash*. Live life to the hilt. The study of philosophy will free you to do that. To become a man."

Leo patted Kiran on the back and guided him out of the interior of the mausoleum down the stairs.

"I'm going to leave you here, if you don't mind," he said, stopping mid-way down the stairs and offering Kiran his hand. "How do you feel?"

"Fine, and thanks." Kiran shook Leo's hand warmly and vigorously. "Thanks *very* much – may I call you Leo?"

"Didn't we already settle that? Of course!" Leo gave him a smile that lit up his heart, then turned and stepped smartly away.

The sun was still high, and Kiran squinted as he stood on the steps of Grant's Tomb. He noticed for the first time two large gilded eagles on either side of the steps. He felt like an eagle himself. All New York lay before him, all the world, the whole universe, compressed into a single short flash. And that flash was benign; Camus had been right after all. Kiran remembered a line from somewhere: "Eternity bores me,/ I never wanted it." Where did it come from? Sylvia Plath, of course. Shalini had recited it to him several times. "I never wanted it." That said it all. The only thing he wanted now, the only thing he would ever want again, was the only thing there was: life here and now. His heart was no longer faint.

But something was nagging at him. Though he knew it was impossible and absurd, he had the weird feeling that Shalini was lurking near-by, just as Leo said. The sense of her presence was almost palpable, and for an instant he shivered at the creepy sensation. He couldn't resist looking over his shoulder to see if she was standing on the stairs above him. Of course he didn't see anything and felt like an idiot.

"I never *wanted* it!" he howled into the vapors of his soulless being.

The strange sensation vanished. He walked briskly down the stairs away from the tomb, away from the ghost of Shalini. He became aware of the rush of traffic around him and the clip-clopping of shoes on the sidewalk. A little boy and his mother clambered into a taxi that had just screeched to a halt. The woman reminded him of the girl his parents had selected for him to marry years before. He remembered how he had stood firm and dashed his parents' hopes. He was feeling like a man.

Chapter 14

I T was not the kind of palpable blackness that sticks to you on a cloudy midnight or that can be bottled up in a darkroom or "cut with a knife." It was more like the darkness of dreams, fainting spells, and ghosts. There were no buildings and no landscape, just a kaleidoscope of shifting shapes, of semi-material lumps drifting like clouds or bumping along like tumbleweeds through the gray mist. Shalini was one of these shapes, a shadow moving through the clammy gloom that was neither night nor day. Only a few days separated her from the deed that took her life, and Kiran, now tucked inside the Whale's Belly, traveled with her through that dark world. With her? No. It would be more accurate to say that he traveled *as* her, feeling the emotions he unleashed in her a quarter century before as his own.

It would not be enough to say that she was confused. Rather she was like someone who has been drugged to the point of stupefaction. She could not remember how she got where she was or what this place was. She could not have told you she was wearing a dirty white smock or lugging around something that looked vaguely like a cello case. Though mysterious things were happening all around her, she could not have asked herself what they were. She had very little idea what she should be doing with her time or why she felt depressed or what had happened to her. Her memory was blunted, and it was only with an effort that she could remember her name. Except at rare intervals she was a nameless point of reference in a dream-like void, an amorphous lump of diffuse feelings with neither willpower nor comprehension.

She was at the mercy of these feelings, which fondled and squeezed and kneaded her like an unseen hand.

Often she heard words that seemed not to belong to her world, and their meanings did not register. They sounded like distant background noise, like street sounds a block away. But occasionally there would be something that stood out, though she did not quite know why. Indeed she could not have asked herself the question, "Why are these words standing out, why are they interesting to me?" But they were interesting nonetheless, and she would note them. She would look up and notice unusually dark shapes from which the words came.

"I heard she wrote down the number of the ambulance," said a voice.

"That's what I heard too. How well did you know her?" said another.

"I would see her in class. I don't think I said more than ten sentences to her. But I admired her. You couldn't help but admire her mind."

"Are you going to the funeral?"

"No, are you?"

"No. I wonder how Kiran is taking it."

In her dazed state she did not understand any of it. But for some reason the conversation made her heart beat fast, and that single word "Kiran" was charged with emotion. It jarred her, it "burned her ears," though she did not know why. She only knew she had to have that word. It materialized in front of her and she snatched it out of the air. She held it, "Kiran," wriggling like a silver fish in her hand. What would she do with it? Ah, a cello case. She would open the case and throw it in. What? An oven! An oven with its mouth gaping open inside the case! The oven had a nightmarish quality; it didn't stay still, and its shape was wobbling. For some reason she was terrified of it, and she dreaded the idea of sticking her hand into it. She threw the word in, slammed the case shut, and turned back to the dark shapes. More words, she wanted more words. She had no idea what she would do with them once she had captured them, but she knew she had to have them. Capturing them, like lugging around the case, was her obsession.

The dark shapes from which the words came were gone, and she picked up her case and moved on through the thick gray mist. How long she walked she could not say. She sometimes dozed along the way – on the way to where? She could not remember. She did not even feel the need to remember. So she dozed, dozed and dreamed. Her dreams were dreams within a larger dream. She barely recognized the difference between that larger, all-inclusive dream that flowed continuously through her drowsy consciousness and the smaller dreams she had when she dozed.

"Let us not pretend that this is not a tragedy. Shalini was a bright and gifted spirit – "

Suddenly, again, Shalini found herself listening. Many dark shapes from that other world were gathered together in some kind of large structure. They were sitting, listening, and there was an oblong box in the middle of them that she felt a nervous, frantic curiosity about. She felt as if some important event were happening, but she did not understand the meaning of it. She seemed to glimpse something out of a remote past that she could not quite remember but that she somehow knew was blessed and precious and lost forever. And it seemed connected with her.

" – and we would all have enjoyed watching her realize her dreams. But there will be time aplenty for her to realize those dreams, and the environment in which this will happen could not be more confused or troubled than the one she left behind and that we are living in now."

What was in that box? And there was one shape in the crowd that particularly interested her. But there were others too, others she almost recognized. Who were they? They were all so familiar, yet strange. But the box. What was in there? She felt drawn to the box and moved closer and closer to it. She looked inside it, looked through the side of the box and saw – what was it? Something inside, a shape, laid out, not like the others. Something strange about the shape. Something different from the other shapes, those mysterious dark shapes. She got right up next to it and looked. She forgot about the other shapes. The odd shape in the box – suddenly it was as if a veil covering it were removed, and she saw the face of a woman. And she recognized it as – no, it couldn't be! A bolt of lightning seemed to flash, and a paroxysm of raw horror blasted her. It was as if a fuse had blown, and she passed out.

She could not have said how long she lay in that swoon. But soon enough she was again shouldering her cello case and moving through the repetitive, gray, shapeless mist. She remembered nothing of that mass of dark shapes, nothing of the woman's face in the box. All she felt was a certain dreamlike sadness. Sometimes she felt overwhelmed by a vague sense that she was lost, but there was no terror associated with it. So diffuse was her awareness that she could not have known what to be terrified of.

"I'm tired of you mooning about the place all the time. Why don't you put her behind you?"

Shalini snapped out of her slumber and looked for the dark shapes in the void overhead. She understood nothing of what was said, but for some reason she was attracted.

"Give me a break, Lisa. It's only been a week. You don't just forget something like that."

"Let's go out. Let's get out of the apartment. You've got to stop blaming yourself. *It wasn't your fault, Kiran!*"

"It wasn't your fault, Kiran" – she had to have those words. She snatched them out of the air and threw open the case. Where was her cello? Ah, the oven! She remembered there had been an oven the time before. She *remembered,* and the fact that she remembered felt like a triumph. There it was, its steely sheen glimmering as it wobbled in the watery air. She walked over to the oven and threw in the words. She did not know what they meant, but she knew she had to have them. They wriggled for a moment, then settled quietly.

She looked back at the dark figures that were talking and forgot about the oven. Feeling a peculiar fascination, she peered closely at the figures, but the harder she peered the less distinct they became. She got up very close, stood right next to them. She concentrated on the words they spoke, mystified by their meaning.

"Shalini might have been half crazy, but in her own crazy way she was – she was brilliant."

She seized on the word "Shalini." It had tremendous power. It was ominous but alluring. She wanted more, still more words.

Suddenly one of the faces became clear. It was colorless, transparent; it looked like the face one sees in a hologram. Then she recognized it. The word "Kiran!" blazed out in front of her like a million neon lights, and the memory of him torpedoed her. She felt all the roiling, tearing emotions of love and hate, but now magnified and uncontrollable, vivid and tactile. Shattered and suffocating, she passed out.

When she woke, all was as before. Murkiness, shadowy movements all around her, and a sense that there was something sinister close to her. There came a moment when she was drawn to two solid black figures in the syrupy, gray fog overhead. These figures seemed to be suspended above her world, like curled up bats glimpsed in deep twilight.

"Leo, a girl killed herself over me about a month ago," said one of the figures, which seemed oddly familiar to her. Again the words fascinated her, and she felt the urge to collect them. For it seemed to her that they contained valuable information. For they had to do with her.

"I dread to think that it might be all a delusion, a delusion for the faint of heart."

Yes, they had to do with her. She felt as if she were being assaulted. She wanted to scream but did not know why.

"What makes you think that? . . . But first tell me, did you love the girl?"

"I thought I did. But no. I cared, I guess. Yeah, I cared. I cared a lot. And it was such a great waste."

"What was her name?"

"Shalini. She was gifted. Very gifted. But fragile."

"And you jilted her."

Important words. Clues. Get them! And get that – the shape of a church came from nowhere into her head. Get it too! She snatched the words out of the fog and then scooped up the church. She carried them over to the case and put down the church to open the case.

Oven! Of course! That thing that was always giving her trouble. She turned to pick up the church, then turned back. The oven was gone! The damn thing! It was all over the place! It had multiplied itself. She threw the church into one of the ovens and the words she had collected into another. Meanwhile more words from the dark figures besieged her. She listened.

"You see, Shalini blackmailed me into coming over to her apartment; it was her birthday; she threatened to kill herself if I didn't come. Lisa got into a snit over this. 'At least be late!' she screamed. She was jealous of Shalini, afraid I would go back to her. 'Don't give her what she wants, at least be late!' she kept saying. I told myself it wouldn't hurt if I was a half hour late, as long as I finally got there. So I caved in. But that half hour was the difference between life and death. She did it with gas."

Shalini could make little sense of what the figures said, but she felt a gamut of emotions connected with them. Some of the words she hated while others felt welcome. Collect them? She had no choice. The words "Lisa" and "Shalini" stood out. The latter she felt inclined to wear as an ornament, a badge of some kind. Was it allowed? Was it? In her confusion the string of words separated into fragments; she watched in despair as they floated disconnectedly into the fog. She began snatching at them randomly. She gathered what she could, moaning as she snatched. Then she saw new words being fashioned.

"This is the only life you'll ever live. 'A flash of light between two eternities of darkness,' said a wise man."

She had little understanding of these new words, but she felt a visceral hatred of them. She felt as if they threatened her with a kind of annihilation, as if their mystery once fathomed would kill her. So strong was her loathing that it overcame her compulsion to collect them. She hated the figure who created them and wished he would go away. The other man, the other man, his were the words she wanted!

"Eternity bores me, I never wanted it," said the man whose words she wanted.

These new words riveted her to him. They reverberated through her whole being. She became an echo chamber, and they echoed in her, touching some extraordinary nerve that fell just short of comprehension.

Without intending it, she found herself so close to the man that she penetrated him. She was inside his dark, solid body, and there are no words to express the delirium of her emotions. First this way then that she turned, like an ant on a suspended stick, both ends burning.

Then everything came clear in an incandescent flash. She knew who the man was. She remembered the oven and the gas and the unspeakable deed. And for the first time she realized, realized with complete clarity – it was the greatest shock of all – that she was dead. A pitiful cry, a whimper, "God help me," dithered out of her mouth. Then the fuse blew, and she passed out.

She did not know how long she lay in that comatose state. But soon enough she was again lugging her cello case through the unending, gray, shapeless fog. She remembered nothing of the face she had seen or the words she had collected. She did not remember she had died or the prayer she said before fainting. She did not remember that there might be an oven in her case instead of a cello. All she felt was a certain dreamlike sadness. Sometimes she felt overwhelmed by a vague sense that she was lost, but there was no terror associated with it. So diffuse was her awareness that she could not have known what to be terrified of.

Chapter 15

A FAINT wind wafted through the chamber. There was something slightly ominous about it, he thought, like the gray, cool wind that blew across the Mandovi as a monsoon squall approached. There was not a sound, just the movement of the air. Kiran was more interested than alarmed by this novelty – until now weather hadn't been a part of Judgment. But he was shocked by what he saw next. There, hovering above him just under the ceiling, was something he recognized. It was the Hindu deity Kala Bhairava, the "Lord of Time," standing in his tiger skin robe. Kala Bhairava was the god that the family priest in Goa spent his whole life worshipping and that Kiran had worshipped too when he was a boy. The deity looked just like the centuries-old image in the family temple, except that now he was alive. His face was black, and squirming little snakes served as earrings, bracelets, and anklets. Bhairava held weapons and severed heads in his four hands.

Very slowly, the god floated downward toward the floor as Kiran looked on in utter amazement. Then the deity fixed a large-eyed stare on Kiran.

When the god didn't speak, Kiran gathered his courage and said, "You are Kala Bhairava, Sir?"

"You may regard me so."

"Why, Sir, do you honor me with – your presence?"

"You will know in due time. I have brought with me a companion. Do you see him?"

Kiran looked up at a form that was being assembled out of the air over Bhairava's head. When it took shape, hovering just under the ceiling, the word *ogre* came to mind, though *demon,* or even *monster,* might have fit it just as well. It was dark red, surrounded by an orange glow the color of flame, and had arms with hulking, veined muscles. Its belly protruded over a loincloth made of an animal pelt, and a necklace of bones hung around its neck. Its body was short and muscular, its face broad and ugly, its glowering eyes vicious, crafty, and incensed. It was close to the most loathsome thing he had ever seen.

"I see it," Kiran said. "Yes, I do see it."

It floated down to the floor and stood next to the god. It breathed; Kiran could see its flanks go in and out.

"It looks like it wants to – it looks menacing," Kiran said.

"Not 'it'. He. He has business with you. You must fight him and defeat him."

"What? How can this be? This is the astral. How can there be violence? We're not physical."

"It's Judgment. Judgment works by its own laws."

"But – but – I'm not a fighter. I'm a teacher, a scholar. What chance would I have against such a being? I would lose for sure. Then what happens?"

"Then you would lose your claim to eternal life."

"To eternal life? But I haven't a chance! I'm no match for it!"

"We shall see. But if you fail, you'll get the reward you promised all your students. Is that not fair?"

This was the most terrible of threats, and Kiran was unprepared for it. Nothing Aaji or his other teachers said hinted at this. But fair?

"Sir, you say it's fair, but I have no chance of beating it. It's an ogre, and I'm a weakling compared to it. How is that fair?"

"Consider how fair your treatment of your students was."

"Yes, I see now that I was in a position of, uh, advantage. I misled them. Yes, I acknowledge that."

"You haven't suffered what you made them suffer. Do you acknowledge *that*?" said the god.

"Yes, but . . . they had a whole life to undo the damage."

"And some have. But others have not. Too often you left behind a legacy of hopelessness. You demolished their faith and left nothing in its place. That was your crime."

"But I was sincere! I did my best with what I had!"

"Did you? Or did you settle for what was fashionable with your set?"

"I *thought* I did my best. That's the way it seemed at the time. But, OK, I grant you have a point. But – I've always deplored violence. I've never even been in a fist fight. Why must I fight in this way? Isn't there some other way? Can we talk it out? Why violence?"

"Don't you know that false views often lead to violence? Even to suicide? Two of your students – "

"Yes, I know, Sir! And I am deeply sorry for that! But do two wrongs make a right? What does more violence accomplish?"

"You argue well, but there are times – rarely – when violence is the only way one learns. The only question that remains is this: How badly do you want eternal life? How much are you willing to suffer for it? And as you fight, fight not only for yourself, but for all the students whose hope you helped destroy. Let them be your inspiration."

"But I – "

At that moment Kala Bhairava disappeared, but his companion didn't.

For the first time, the ogre spoke. "Fight," it said in a gravelly voice.

"Do you have a name?" said Kiran, still not convinced there was no other way. "Do you really want to carry through with this? Let's talk. Let's reason it out."

The monster's only response was to go into a wrestler's crouch and raised its arms, its fingers distended. Its tongue, fat and oily, lolled out, and its eyes blazed red.

Kiran backed away as it advanced toward him. He felt the wall behind. A galloping prayer addressed to anything that might be in range rushed out of him. He studied the ogre, and the ogre gazed back at him. "Look at me," it snarled. "This is how you would look if you hadn't hidden your dark side so skillfully. This is the body you deserved on earth. Study it, Kiran Kulkarni. See yourself as you are!"

Kiran was amazed that the thing spoke with intelligence. Perhaps it could be reasoned with after all. He knew the accusation was true in one sense, and pleaded, "As I *was*. Not as I am!"

The thing stopped, a look of puzzlement on its ugly face. Then it looked with renewed menace and growled, "Prove it, Kiran Kulkarni! If you are right, you will win. But if you are wrong . . ."

The ogre moved another step toward him in its crouch, and Kiran knew that all his argumentative skills were useless. He would have to use physical force. He couldn't see how he could win, but then he remembered what Bhairava said: "Fight not only for yourself, but for all your students." By God, he would do just that! He would fight for all those students he wounded! For the first time he really cared for them. He grieved over what he had done to them – perhaps to their children down through the generations. Suddenly his body's strength grew. A barbarian power lodged in his muscles, a warrior's courage rose up in him. He lunged at the ogre.

As a high god and the king of demons in one of India's great epics duel for days on end, first one and then the other gaining the advantage, so Kiran and the ogre fought on. Hitting, kicking, twisting, biting, strangling, singeing, scratching, gouging, flinging, jumping, spitting, shouting – every strategy open to combatants not carrying weapons was used. When Kiran found himself pinned or being strangled, he saved himself by remembering the penalty for losing. He might lose, but he would not surrender eternal life, for himself or his students, without a heroic effort. When he had the advantage, the ogre seemed to gather strength for a counterattack from a desire to send him to oblivion. Each was mastered by a supreme passion.

Kiran had never known much physical pain on earth. And it wasn't supposed to be even possible on an astral planet. But Judgment was obviously different. He could see hunks of his flesh lying on the floor as he slogged through the gore, and the corresponding holes in his body felt like giant thorns. Every encounter with the ogre's fiery breath, which had singed his head and neck, inflicted more pain. When the ogre hammered out his front teeth, the thought of his ugliness hurt almost as much. And when it gouged out his right eye, his horror at going eyeless hurt as much as the wound itself.

At the same time he felt exhilarated. At first he didn't know where it came from, but it was as pronounced as the pain. As the battle wore on, he began to understand. He was locked in a death struggle with all that was evil in him, and the gaining of the advantage against it thrilled him. He noticed something else. The ogre's appearance had gradually changed. It became less ugly, smaller, weaker, less threatening, less angry. Its color changed from red to tan. The word "ogre" didn't fit anymore. Now it looked human.

The advantage went to Kiran more and more as the fight wore on, but he couldn't deliver the blow that would end it. Time and again he would have his enemy pinned down and all but strangled when somehow he would get loose. But finally the moment came. Kiran summoned all his strength in a final blow to the head. The enemy finally lay dead.

Kiran jumped back from the disfigured body. He half expected it to move again, but it didn't. Nothing in the whole gory mess around him moved except – what was that? Kiran leaned over and saw – it was pink and meaty, it looked like a tongue. Yes, that's what it was. He remembered he'd torn out the monster's tongue in a rage after he'd lost his eye – was it days or weeks before? Like an elephant's trunk severed from its body in battle, it twitched and writhed in death with a life of its own. Kiran stomped on it over and over, as if it were a snake, until it, too, finally lay still.

For a few moments he savored his triumph, but then he grew thoughtful. He recognized the justice in being forced to fight and destroy the symbol of all that was evil in him, right down to the severed tongue, the thing he wielded with such deadly effect on earth.

"The Ordeal is good," he said aloud. And then, to no one in particular, "Thank you." He was overcome by the beauty, the utter rightness, of it all.

But only for a moment. Like a wind-driven fire consuming everything in its path, the pain of his wounds rose up and overwhelmed him, and he lost consciousness.

When he woke, he found himself in the same Whale's Belly he had started in. It was clean and tidy. He next realized that he, too, was clean and – he felt himself all over – *reconstructed*. He was elated. And then a third surprise: An apparition glowed in front of him in the round. Like Bhairava and the ogre, she was real, living, not a projection on the screen. He thought he recognized her from somewhere. She half-smiled at him.

"Congratulations, Kiran Kulkarni," she said, "you have come through Judgment with flying colors. Well done!" Then she said dryly, as if enjoying an insider's joke, "You get an A+."

"Is it really over? Over at last? Nothing else I have to do?"

"You never wavered throughout the whole ordeal. You never asked for a furlough. You never quit. Wonderful for you!"

"Yes, it *is* wonderful. . . . But who are you? And why do I get the impression I know you from somewhere? Have we met?"

"No, but you may have seen my photograph. On earth I was a philosopher and novelist and non-believer like you. That's why I volunteered to be your priestess. My name was – is – Iris Murdoch."

"Iris Murdoch! Really! You were my priestess? I am honored! So you guided me through the ordeal, all of it? But – "

"Every second of it. And more of it than you suspect."

"What do you mean?"

"Get ready for a surprise. I was Kala Bhairava."

"What?!"

"I fashioned my body after something I knew you would recognize and honor – and feel somewhat comfortable with."

"So Kala Bhairava was just an illusion?"

"Yes and no. I was really inside the body you saw. It wasn't an empty hologram. Can you forgive me?" She smiled mischievously.

He mused in silence for a few moments and took stock, then said, "And what about the ogre? Was that an illusion? And the threat that I would become nothing? I didn't think you *could* become nothing."

"You can't. Even if you'd lost the battle, you wouldn't have become nothing. I took a risk. You could even say I lied. But I lied to help you develop compassion for the students you misled – I misled mine, and thousands of my readers as well. My priest threatened me with nothingness, too. That was just a few months ago."

"What about the ogre? He felt awfully real! But he wasn't, was he?"

"Oh yes he was. On earth he was a boxer. In one of his fights he cheated and left his opponent a paraplegic. He wanted to experience this disability as much as he could. He begged me to help him, and I thought of you. While you were fighting to win, he was fighting to lose – and get dreadfully beaten up in the process. Underneath that tough exterior there is a sensitive soul eager to progress."

"So you are a counselor of sorts."

"No. Just a priestess – until my next assignment. I hope to be a Solomon."

"Fascinating. I wonder what *my* future holds."

"Whatever it is, may it take you forward – forward into worlds realer than Eidos. We were both blinded by appearances back on earth, weren't we? Stay in touch, Kiran Kulkarni. You're free to go. Use the door."

And with that she disappeared.

Chapter 16

EIDOS welcomed Kiran home a second time. He marveled again at the immense astral planet's universal symbols linking all its sectors, with billions of souls from a thousand different cultures able to communicate with each other. This telepathic meta-language made possible a society only dreamed of on earth – it seemed much more awe-inspiring to him now than when he first came over at death. You could experience San Francisco, New York, London, Paris, Rome, Kyoto, New Delhi, Beijing, Buenos Aires, Jerusalem, Cairo, Johannesburg, Chiang Mai, and Machu Picchu at a moment's notice, and without the language barrier or the pollution or the waits or the bad weather. Everywhere there was high-spirited banter and debate about astral art and music. You could attend any of the many "athletic" events. You could enjoy current fashions, mental contests and games, historical theater. Lectures and classes on science and religion abounded. And there were endless debates over the best ways to bring souls out of the Shadows. There were trips – guided tours – to the planet's pleasanter places, especially its natural, unspoiled landscapes. All in all the afterworld, with its dense nucleus Earth, was spectacular. And to think that *earth* knew almost nothing of it, its vibratory pulse unsensed by Earth's finest instruments!

Eidos was just one small sector of this vast planet, and it was Kiran's home. Now he really did feel at home there. With the Judgment behind him he was a "graduate," a "regular," and that was a good feeling. But Eidos was no vacation spa. It was true it made him almost giddy with its beauty, and the living Light felt like a great motherly presence swaddling him in its unwavering good will. But since his "briefing" with Aaji and Ganesh following the official welcome after Judgment, or "homecoming," he felt almost oppressed by the prospect of work – yes, work, for loafing in Eidos was not allowed after Judgment. "New challenges" – that's the way Aaji had put it. Hadn't she described the Judgment the same way? He thought of life back on dense earth and missed it a little.

His mind turned to the briefing with his grandfather as Ganesh felt him out about the work he wanted to do. Would he like to welcome souls who had been scoffers like himself when they died? They could use a lot of help, Ganesh had said. The right word might save them from a stay in the Shadowlands and lead them to the Light, where they might slowly adjust. Or would he like to train as a priest and do for others what Iris had done for him? Or how about entering one of the schools to search out new truths among fellow philosophers and eventually become a teacher? There were many seminars exploring the nature of the knowing Light that surrounded and interpenetrated the planet, some of them taught by beings from higher worlds. Would that interest him? Another topic of near universal interest was the relation between the various planes of being and the many different sectors within each plane. Where, exactly, did Eidos fit in? What was its unique significance? What changes did it need to make? Always there was curiosity about the higher worlds inhabited by more advanced, generally happier beings. What did it take to get there? And was there ever an end to the soul's progress as it climbed the ladder toward greater enlightenment? Did it lose its identity as a distinct entity when and if it ever reached that end? Did it even merge with the Light? And what was to be done about the countless billions living in the Shadowlands? How could these dark realms be depopulated without contaminating the worlds of Light? Did he find any of this interesting enough to train as a teacher specializing in one of these areas? Ganesh asked. Kiran wasn't sure.

There were seminars on every conceivable topic. Teachers specialized in ethereal physics, interworld politics, the Islamic astral sector, Eidosian entertainment, the harnessing of dark energy for earth's future needs, even global warming. And there was the Einstein circle. Einstein hypothesized that astral matter was the same thing that earthlings were calling dark matter. They were the visible and invisible sides of the same thing. But it was said he was having trouble with the math needed to prove it.

"Does any of this sound interesting to you?" Ganesh asked. "Just because you weren't trained as a scientist on Earth doesn't mean you can't cultivate new interests here, even eventually become a teacher or team leader. What do you say?"

Somehow teaching didn't appeal to him.

Kiran was left with the impression that Eidos was one vast training ground where industry and curiosity were prized above everything else, and sloth was the cardinal sin.

But this was not true. "Actually the most important thing here is love; it sounds corny, doesn't it?" Ganesh told him during another of their talks. "Then follows work – actually work, ideally, is the active way of expressing love. Then everything else."

One day during one of their talks on the porch facing out toward the river, Ganesh gave Kiran a surprising lesson in the family history. "Madhavi and I, your Aaji and I, were not happy together on earth – did you know that?"

"No? Really? I – can this really be true?""

"It was odd," said Ganesh. "I disapproved of her terribly. She was headstrong and undisciplined, flighty, intent on being silly, not at all serious. For a while I kept my displeasure to myself. I hoped that by mildness and subtlety I could bring her around to more dignified behavior. Finally I couldn't stand it any longer, and I started telling her exactly how I felt until I became excessively picky. For a while we fought openly. We disgraced ourselves in front of the servants. For most of our marriage I thought I'd made a terrible mistake, but once she knew I was dying she became serious and tender – altogether changed. And beautiful in her newfound dignity. In other words, I was no sooner dead than she became the person I needed her to be. Isn't that just like life on earth?" Ganesh laughed, then continued: "When we met after her death – this was in one of the Hindu sectors before we came over here to Eidos, first me, then her – I couldn't help but treat her with coolness. I knew she had changed, but old habits die hard, and I wouldn't let myself trust her. But she persisted and eventually won my trust – actually not too long ago, at about the time you came over. She turned out to be my salvation. I was a loner here, a recluse who would go to school, then apply the lessons in chilly isolation. Eventually I became known as a teacher; I specialized in preparing those getting ready to reenter flesh. But I had no intimate friends, I was standoffish. Then Madhavi came back into my life – after almost fifty years! She brought me warmth and joy for the first time. I love her now more than I can tell."

"Aaji's never said a word about all this," Kiran said. "Isn't that surprising? I'm thinking back. I've always had the impression from what she's said that you gave her more than she gave you. I'm sure if I asked her now she'd say so."

"That's because she thinks with her heart!" Ganesh laughed. "Which, by the way, is usually the best way to think, the way that cool-headed intellectuals like us find so hard over here! But sometimes objectivity has its advantages. No, *I* owe her more."

Objective or not, Kiran knew Ganesh was wrong about one thing. Ganesh was no mere "cool-headed intellectual." Kiran wondered where his grandfather's calm, strangely loving glance came from. He wanted to have a glance like that, to feel what was behind the glance.

After a lot of consulting, Kiran's teachers and guardians decided what to recommend. He and Ganesh sat on the screened porch in their usual chairs. Ganesh had been chosen to deliver the "Assignment."

It came in two parts.

"Your mother-in-law, Velma Stein, died while you were in Judgment," said Ganesh, dressed as usual in his unpretentious beige shirt. "I know you despised her back on earth."

"God help her!" said Kiran explosively, half out of pity and half revulsion.

"She's in trouble. You'll remember she was an alcoholic. She still is – we don't leave our habits behind just because we die, as you know. Only now she's operating from deep within the Shadows and hangs around drunks back on earth. She gets inside their bodies and imagines she *is* them. Her will is tenacious, desperate, she's living as a parasite. And she's working a lot of mischief on the people back on earth she drinks through. But someday out of her agony she'll call for help. I can't think of any greater challenge for you, no better opportunity to practice the universal compassion you must cultivate here. You'll need to keep a steady eye on her and nudge her in the right direction. In effect you'll serve as her guardian; her former guardians all gave up on her, and she's unprotected – a dangerous state to be in. When she calls, or rather *if* she calls, be there for her. In the meantime you'll attend school to learn how to go about it. It won't be pleasant at first; to tell you the truth it will never be. But it's *necessary*. It teaches lessons you can't learn in any other way. And it could become a labor of love. It will become that to the degree you abolish self-will."

Velma had despised him as much as he despised her, and now he was expected to do this for her? Back on earth he had kept away from her. And now he would have to look after her like – like a nursemaid – or so he supposed. He felt a shiver of disgust, but he didn't object.

"Your other job would be to help Shalini," Ganesh said after a pause.

Shalini. Now that could be more interesting.

"By the way, do you remember where you left her?"

"You mean in that Bronx apartment, in that earth dream – or should I call it a nightmare?"

"Yes. Well, that was a nice place compared to where she is now. We hadn't wanted to tell you this, but she's deeper in the shadows than ever. She lives in the Shadowlands of astral Vatican, the largest of the Catholic worlds. She spends her time never moving more than a few yards, crouched under a bush. We haven't taken you there yet. Vatican's "basement," as we call it – it's an immense world in itself with over a hundred million inhabitants. It's a murky, rather chilly place. A dull world lacking color and sunlight, just like our Shadowland, only ours is much smaller – that's because our overall population is smaller. She looks comatose to outer appearance. She just sits. She pities or blames or justifies herself in her imagination. She relives old memories, the same ones over and over, endlessly, or imagines horrible scenes, scenes out of Dante. She's lost in her personal hell. She's unreachable, doesn't talk to anyone. It's a ghastly business, but it can't go on forever. The Creator loves us all too much for that to happen – or so we tell ourselves. But on the other hand the Creator isn't going to get us out of our scrapes if we don't even try to help each other! Maybe you can do something, Kiran. No one else has been able to, not even her grandparents or other relatives. Maybe because you care more for her than they do. Or maybe because you have a will of iron and are in the habit of seeing things through to the finish. Well, what do you say?"

"To tell you the truth, it sounds like a challenge I might like. At least it beats the heck out of watching over Velma Stein!"

"You would have to do both, you understand. The two jobs go together."

"Oh Lord! OK."

"Let me warn you. Shalini is quite out of her mind. We would call her insane. Once she loses all control, *all* control . . . the truth is she's very close, hazardously close, to entering earth 'end over end' as we say. We can't let this happen. She's come too far for that."

"End over end? Do you mean as an animal?"

"A possibility in the most extreme cases. For her, probably not that dire. Maybe she would be born to parents too poor to educate her properly. That at best. Or in some crime-infested neighborhood where she would probably be raped. The possibilities are endless. We want her to have a decent birth. We think she deserves it."

Aaji came through the door, and Ganesh looked at her as if welcoming help. "For many," Aaji said as she took her place in the rocker, "any form of guided rebirth is a blessing."

"Your mission is to break into her world," Ganesh continued, "as assertively as we are allowed – and do your best to lead her to freedom. You'll be appalled by what you see. Completely appalled. I cannot stress this enough. Not even her old guardian Sylvia Plath could save her this time. Watching your mother-in-law will teach you new tricks. Shalini will force you to use old ones. The rigor and creativity you brought to problem-solving back on earth might serve you well. I hope so. We will have to see."

"One last thing, my dear boy," Aaji added. "Keep a sense of perspective about all this. You'll probably fail time and again. Don't be too hard on yourself. She might not be progressing, but *you* will be. Bounce back, talk to your teacher, talk to us, take in a concert or go to a museum with a friend, meditate and pray, play a game, and try again."

"And, of course, you can decline this assignment. Or you can quit mid-course. You're always free to do something else," added Ganesh. "But you must do *something*."

"Right. But will I be taught how to deal with her?"

"A crash course, one-on-one, from a master of intrusive intervention," said Ganesh. "His name is Nigel. He was an English detective back on earth. You can begin at once if you like; he's expecting you. Or you can enter her world, or try to, even before you're ready. You'll see quickly what you're up against. There isn't really any perfect training for this sort of thing. No rules are guaranteed to work. Only love works in the long run. Sorry!"

Walking along the beach later that day, Kiran thought of the last time he saw Shalini. He remembered how she yelled at him, "I despise you!" but also her final desperate call, "Don't leave me!" He was excited. Shalini would be a huge challenge, and he told himself he was ready for it. All the duties of guardianship, meditation and prayer, unity and fellow feeling, loving one's neighbor as oneself – these were things that were good and necessary, but they didn't come easy to him. But Shalini was a person he really cared for. What had happened to her? What could he do for her that not even Sylvia Plath could do? He felt flattered. So he really *had* learned some useful skills back on earth. "Rigor," Ganesh had called it. So there was a place for it here. He beamed.

His thoughts turned to rebirth. "A blessing," Aaji had said, as long as it was guided. He wondered if someday it might be a "blessing" for him. The thought unsettled him. Reincarnation meant that one and the same person could have different bodies, different brains, even a different sex. He still didn't like the idea of surrendering his current personality. There was no telling what sort of body and brain he might end up with. Too risky! He turned his mind back to Shalini.

Chapter 17

THE detachment Kiran had cultivated in difficult stints of meditation fled in a moment. No training could have prepared him for this.

Nigel led him into a middle sector of the Shadowlands – a twilight sector higher than the dark, indescribable horrors of the "true hells," as they were called – and there was Shalini by her bush. Sitting beside her, he entered her earth dream with ease, for he had done it once before. In it she was sitting on the floor of the apartment where he'd left her. She wore dirty shorts and a raggedy shirt streaked with red paint that looked like it belonged to an artist. Her feet were folded in, her knees splayed out. Her tangled hair was streaked and caked with filth, and there were scratch marks down her arms. Piled neatly on bookshelves, cabinets, and sideboards which lined the wall on all four sides, the polished bones of animals arranged by species and type gleamed. The room had become an ossuary. Several living animals – mostly cats, rabbits, guinea pigs, and a small dog – sniffed and scurried from room to room of her imaginary world.

With knife in hand and a glassy-eyed, unblinking, strangely innocent stare, she was pinning down a tabby cat to the floor with a nail through each paw as she sang a child's song. The cat yowled and with its two free paws clawed Shalini's wrists. Kiran flinched as he felt by mental osmosis the lacerating though imaginary pain from the scratches, but he also felt something vaguely like satisfaction, though whether from inflicting or receiving pain he couldn't tell.

He wanted to step in and put an end to the ritual, but he remembered Nigel's warning never to interfere beyond a certain point "lest you become a possessing demon." He reminded himself the animal was real only in Shalini's imagination and that she was the only real sufferer, and what suffering she felt was, in the last analysis, purely emotional, not physical – like his during the battle with the ogre. The scratches on her body were no more real than the nails through the cat's paws. He stood and watched, still unseen, unfelt, as the torture proceeded. He couldn't have said whether he felt more disgust or pity.

He decided to confront her. He sat down in front of her as the half-crucified cat flailed its legs in the air between them. "Shalini," he said mentally in the universal language of the afterworld. Then again, "Shalini," but this time aloud in English.

She didn't look up. He realized he made no dent on her consciousness.

He closed his eyes and concentrated on her, trying to break through the barrier Nigel had warned him of.

She looked up with large, vacant, unrecognizing eyes. She looked like a zombie. "Sweetly, sweetly I breathe in," she said, humming a little tune and staring straight through him. "Sweetly, sweetly," she repeated.

He felt a flicker of recognition in her, a glimpse of something out of a remote past she couldn't quite remember but somehow knew was blessed and precious and lost forever. "Sweetly, sweetly," she mumbled, the same phrase flitting again and again through her dazed mind.

Then he felt her mood change. Picking up her claw hammer, she stopped singing and applied herself to the task at hand with sadistic vigor. The cat yowled and tried to scratch her with its one remaining paw, but it failed, and the paw wobbled pathetically in the air.

Calling up all his energy, he tried to penetrate her subconscious to learn what all the animals and bones symbolized. No one thing, it seemed. Did they represent all things? He knew this couldn't be, for no one, according to Nigel, was so far gone that she hated all things. He had come up against his limits. He retreated out of the shadows back to brilliant Eidos.

"You can reach her only through a symbol that you both understand, that will sharpen her focus and give you some purchase on her state of mind," Nigel said at their next meeting.

"Any suggestions?" said Kiran.

"Well, can you think of something she truly hated or feared? Feared above everything else she ever came across. Something that will slap her sharply in the face and bring her out of her trance. It could be an event. Or an object. Something that would make her feel real terror or disgust."

"How about *me*?" said Kiran.

"No, no. Her feelings for you are completely ambivalent."

"I'll have to think about it."

"Think carefully," said Nigel. "Think carefully and see if it doesn't leap out at you."

Shalini, dressed this time in a dirty dress, was carefully arranging bones along the shelves, as if she were a librarian in a rare books room. He studied her movements for a clue. "Something that will slap her sharply in the face" – what in the world could that be? He didn't know whether to look for it in the imaginary arrangement of the furniture, the clothing she wore, her appearance, the mutterings coming from her mouth, or the techniques of torture she used. He was open to any possibility but still had no clue.

He walked into the kitchen, opened drawers and cupboard doors, tested the spigots, checked the refrigerator to see what food might be on hand. Then he noticed there was a gap, a vacant space along the wall between the counters. What did the kitchen lack? A stove. The gap was where the stove should be. He saw the gas outlet on the wall and remembered Shalini's suicide. He wondered if the gap was important. He would bring back the information to Nigel.

Coming out of the kitchen into the ossuary, he tried again to penetrate Shalini's consciousness, and again he managed to distract her slightly from her task. She stopped straightening up her bones and turned toward the center of the room. He felt a vague, melancholy sensation, but he couldn't establish communication. He waved his arm and called out "Shalini!" But nothing he did with his body registered. Only his mind as it concentrated had an effect, a very slight one.

He stood and waited for her to do something. With the same glassy, round-eyed, unblinking stare, she began creeping along behind a white rabbit. With lightning quickness she sprang, seized the squealing animal, and gathered it into her hands.

Kiran walked into the bedroom and began going through the dresser drawers and closet. There was almost nothing; the dirty shorts she wore were apparently her Sunday best.

On the way out he screamed at her at the top of his lungs. She didn't hear a thing. Already she had disemboweled the rabbit and was cutting it up. It was obvious she had undergone some horrible trauma. Was it her suicide, or was it what let up to it? Or was it both? Or was it something else? Whatever it was, it was obvious to Kiran that her tender soul was frozen. He was losing confidence he could thaw it out.

Nigel couldn't make much sense of the new information, but Sylvia Plath, who dropped in from time to time to help, had spent nearly twelve earth years herself in Eidos's Shadows following her own suicide. She had closely followed Shalini's sad, up-and-down plight, and for a time became her spirit guide. A hopeless task, as it turned out.

"You say there was an absent stove in the kitchen?" Plath asked. It was clear she was intrigued. "This is a new development, it was there the last time I visited, but that was years ago. I wonder if its disappearance has something to do with you. Maybe she's more aware of you than it seems. I wonder." She paused, then added: "Next time you go to her, why don't you create a stove with an oven, one that looks like the one back in that Bronx apartment? Maybe that's what you're looking for. Maybe *that* will jolt her back."

"Just a minute. Are you saying I can help her create her imaginary world? I can add the stove to her earth dream by *imagining* it?"

"Hmm, yes," said Nigel. "You share the dream. You are an active participant. But you're not allowed to force anything on her she doesn't really want. That's against the law. But you can throw it out there for her to consider. Nothing wrong with that."

"Maybe that's exactly the symbol you've been looking for," Plath repeated.

For a moment no one spoke as they mulled over the strange solution that Plath came up with. Then she said to Kiran, "And how are you holding up? Not too pleasant, eh? The Shadows, I mean."

"Not pleasant at all. And to think that I almost ended up there!"

"Like me! But there came a point when I stopped pitying myself, and that was the beginning."

It was a brilliant idea, and Kiran admired Plath for coming up with it. But he saw something else he didn't admire so much. For a moment he stared at her refined, ironic eyes and felt her imperfect compassion for Shalini, her determined but uninspired commitment to Shalini's wellbeing, as if she were a novel that the writer had lost interest in but had to complete anyway. Commitment, that's what it was, no more and no less. Noble, but not inspired. He realized Plath was a long way from the kind of insight that made compassion easy and natural, but, then, so was he. He felt their alikeness: two souls struggling to dim down the selfish ego, to give birth to that most exquisite and difficult perception, unity. Did she experience the same tedium, the same failure? He was sure she did.

Then he realized more completely – for the first time really – why he had been given the task of bringing Shalini back. It was true: he loved Shalini, really and truly cared for her. No one else cared as much – sad, but true. He brought to the task a sincerity and fervor no one else could. Suddenly he felt uplifted and purified and empowered by this love. He almost believed he would succeed.

Shalini primped in front of the mirror in her bedroom. Had she bathed? She wore a fresh blue-green bathrobe, and there were no quills of blood-matted hair sticking out of her head, like a porcupine three days dead on the roadside. Kiran took heart in this new development as he entered her mind's world.

Into the "kitchen" he went, pulled up one of the two chairs, and concentrated on the act of creating.

It required the kind of concentration that in more developed souls resulted in houses. For him it was turning out to be a difficult and imperfect labor – he was certainly no astral artisan! He tried to put the stove in the gap between the counters, but this was proving difficult. Every time he was about to succeed, the space in the gap narrowed. Finally the stove stayed put, though there was something about it that made him think of a child's drawing. But there it was, a stove with an oven, and it occupied the correct space. Though he felt a little silly, he couldn't help admiring the clumsy facsimile, for he had never done anything like this before. Even back on earth he had been a lousy artist, so what could he expect? Nevertheless, it was made in the service of another. One might even say it was made out of love. Take away the background of unity, however imperfect, take away his willing participation in Shalini's fantasy, and the creation would fail to adhere in her imaginary world.

He decided to take some bones from their shelves in the living room to the kitchen table. She would look for them in the kitchen, where he hoped she would notice his creation. He was excited when he closed the door to her earth dream and left her alone.

When he checked in on her a little later, he was tense with excitement. He was sure that something in Shalini's inner world must have changed. He caught himself walking on tiptoe as he entered her world.

He couldn't believe it. The bones were not where he left them in the kitchen, and the oven he had squeezed into its space was gone. He went into the living room and found the bones back on their shelf. But no oven. Stepping around Shalini, who sat staring into space doing nothing, he searched the whole apartment. The oven had vanished.

"OK," said Nigel when they regathered, "you failed for now. But don't give up. Put the thing *in her face,* right in front of her, wherever you find her. And if that doesn't work, turn on the jets so she can smell the gas! What the hell! Why not?" Kiran could tell that Nigel was frustrated. He was like a doctor facing the death of his patient after he's done all he can.

"I'll try it, but maybe we're on the wrong track. Maybe there just isn't anything we can do. Maybe her return to reality can't be rushed," said Kiran.

"Then God help her! What a waste!"

Kiran reentered her world, and there she was, sorting out her bones, counting them, like a miser counting her coins. Again her appearance was unkempt. New scratch marks – deep ones, more like cuts, even gashes – stood out red and angry on her back. He watched with a sick feeling as she dug a small skeletal cat's claw into her wrist, her face never changing its catatonic expression. How horrible: to use the animal she loved best to inflict the wound on her body! He attuned himself to her mind and felt the usual loathing.

This time he didn't just place the oven in its space with his imagination. He first imagined himself carrying the thing in his arms. He would place the thing in front of her as if he, and it, were physically right there.

He didn't know what would happen when he set the thing down. Would she see it even then? And even if she did, what reason did he have to think something constructive would happen?

But she did see it, and for the first time since he began working with her, her expression took on animation. Her eyes became even rounder than they ordinarily were in their stare, and her eyes blinked and fluttered; color came back into her face. A tremendous force seemed to enter her. Her mouth flew open, and out of it came the most unbelievable volume of sound, a scream for the ages. Bones began falling off the shelves, first only a few, then more, then an avalanche.

Kiran felt exhilaration. It worked! But then, like flames jumping a fire break, her suffering swept him up, and he did the equivalent of fainting. He found himself back in Aaji's presence, back in Aaji's house.

"What? You left her? You must go back at once! Go! Go!" That is all Aaji had time to say as she physically pushed him out of her sight.

Nigel's forehead wrinkled. He began to speak, then shifted in his chair and looked out the back window across the lawn into an English garden. "How are you holding up now?" he said with compassion.

"Pretty horrible," said Kiran. "Being in her mind is like fighting that ogre in the Belly. Other than that, not bad!" he chuckled. Then he added more seriously: "Actually I'm encouraged. The bones are still there, but they're cluttering her apartment; they stay where they fall. She's not polishing or arranging them anymore. And I didn't see any animals last time. And, as I told you, she's re-imagined her apartment around the oven, with the thing in its proper place in the kitchen."

Kiran grew sober and said, "And she remembers her death, the whole terrible mess that led up to it, and the memories don't drive her out of her mind anymore. It's funny, Nigel, but I admire her. Only a perfectionist, someone who truly cares about getting things right and making amends, could subject herself to so much torment. Only a deep and sensitive spirit could punish herself so much. There's something admirable about it."

"The sages say great evil is always a perversion of great good," said Nigel.

"And I owe her something," Kiran went on. "I'm sure it's a mark of my immaturity, but working with her is the most interesting thing about Eidos for me. I live more intensely in her orbit. She's like a tonic."

"By colliding with her you help define yourself," Nigel said.

"Why? Am I not defined enough already?"

At that moment Nigel's daughter Myrna manifested in a simple white dress. She and Nigel looked the same age. She was a radiantly healthy forty, but the light shining from her had a more spiritual sheen than her father's. She said she had just returned from work "in the trenches" (a term referring to the Shadows), then excused herself.

"Is she comfortable here?" said Kiran.

"Very. She's been in Eidos for only three years and feels none of the pull of earth that you and I feel. Her Judgment was short and untraumatic. How long was yours, by the way?"

"Forty-three days, they tell me."

"My God! And I thought mine was long!"

"It felt like an eternity."

"Well, on earth she was devoted to her family. Lucky for her she married a man who didn't take advantage of that devotion. As a matter of fact, when she died at fifty-two of breast cancer, her two children were already grown, and her husband became a monk. In her previous life she was a male who lived into his seventies – again upright I'm told."

"Really! Another who finishes her earth cycle as a woman!" said Kiran. "Aaji won't go back either. I wonder if there are statistics. Do more finish the cycle as man or woman? Do you know?"

"There are statistics, and slightly more women do," said Nigel, "exactly the reverse of what India's sages back on earth teach. But of course that tradition was developed by males!"

Kiran enjoyed Nigel. They were peers in terms of comfort in Eidos. Both of them were run-of-the-mill souls at their present stage of development. They ranked in the "middle percentiles" among the regular inhabitants of Eidos (those who had undergone Judgment). For them Eidos was more purgatorial than heavenly; they were still driven mainly by selfish desires and pleasures. Though they might stay in Eidos and grit it out, they were ripe for rebirth on earth. Since they had undergone Judgment, they had earned the right to control what family they would be born into, a very great advantage. It was this advantage they wanted for Shalini.

Kiran reflected on the contrast between Shalini and the serene Myrna. Had he been given a project certain to fail? Had he been given it *because* it was certain to fail? Sometimes he thought so. But in the main he didn't resent it, and he didn't feel discouraged. By now he completely trusted Ganesh and Aaji to provide him the proper lessons, and if watching Shalini fail carried a lesson for him, then let it be. Yet it hurt him to think of Shalini failing. With all his heart he wanted her to be happy.

Chapter 18

SHALINI wondered why the man kept doing nice things for her. Why did he bring her flowers? Why did he buy her a beautiful new sari or blouse? Why did he sit beside her next to her bush and read poetry aloud? Why did he look so tenderly at her? He looked like Kiran and he had the feel of Kiran as far as she could remember him. He even insisted that he *was* Kiran. But he didn't act like Kiran. Whoever he was, what did he see in her? What kind of a man would make such a fuss over her? She had killed herself, she was the rubble of the afterworld. She didn't dare show her face to anyone, yet this man acted as if he cared for her. Sometimes she found herself seduced into thinking he really did care, but she would catch herself in time and remember with twin stabs in the heart the real Kiran Kulkarni, the one who rejected her twice. She would sit beside her bush and stare out at the comings and goings of other spirits like herself and remember the price of loving too much.

There he was again, the fool. He was coming all the time now, coming into the Shadows with its murky daylight and parched brown earth to see her.

"Sylvia Plath sends greetings," he said.

She remembered with a twinge of guilt the last time she saw her old mentor. She had literally thrown her out of the apartment. That was before her latest binge of animal torture. "Oh God, all those cats! Let me get away from those memories!" she said.

"Shalini, they weren't *real*," the man who looked like Kiran said, "you were just torturing *yourself*, you were projecting yourself out into them and torturing yourself. You don't have to do that anymore. Let me show you another way."

The fool was at it again! But such a sweet fool, and so like Kiran.

"I *am* Kiran," said the man, "and I care deeply about you."

No, he couldn't be Kiran, Kiran didn't care, Kiran rejected her. Twice.

"Shalini, you're a wonderful person, if only you could accept it," he said.

Of course she couldn't accept it, but it made her feel happy to hear him say it even if he was a fool.

The silly fool had carried in a rug, a beautiful rug of Persian design. "I brought this for you," he said. He began unfurling it across the ground under her bush. She felt confused.

But this momentary confusion didn't make her forget her purpose now that "Kiran" had come. She had searched her past and devised a test for the fool, the amiable trickster, the man who pretended to be Kiran Kulkarni. She would test him now as he unfurled the rug.

"If you are Kiran, who was your wife back on earth?" she began.

"Lisa," said the man, looking up at her from his crouched position with surprise and a look of confusion.

"If you are Kiran, what school did you attend when we dated?"

"School? Fordham."

She saw a strange light in his eyes as he put the last flap of the rug down and carefully positioned himself in front of her. She felt he was eager to participate in the quiz. Why would that be? She wondered how he knew the answers. But the hard questions she had saved for last. She would trip him up yet.

"Along what river did I live?"

"The Hudson."

"What was the topic of the class I gave?"

"Sylvia Plath, Shalini! Keep going!" Intense excitement lit up his face. He appeared to guess what she was doing.

She was frightened. She had never believed the man was Kiran, indeed she had never realized how certain she was that he wasn't until now when it dawned on her that he really might be. She felt wobbly inside, excited, hopeful, vulnerable – above all vulnerable. She didn't think there was a chance the man would pass her quiz. She began to hope he would, but the tough questions were still ahead.

"If you are Kiran, then you will be able to tell me what music we made love to."

"Let me think. Mozart."

"Which Mozart?"

"Clarinet. It's been so long. There was a clarinet, that's all I can remember."

"Was it a concerto, a sonata, a trio, a quartet, a quintet, a – ?"

"Quintet! The clarinet quintet! That's it!"

Oh my God! Was it really Kiran? But there was one more question. If only he could answer it. She shuddered to think that he might.

"If you are Kiran, then you will be able to tell me the name of your car, the name I gave it."

"The Mormal!" he bellowed. "The MORMAL! A name out of Chaucer!"

She looked intently into his face, his eager, caring face, the face she had dubbed "the fool" and "the pretender," and said, "Kiran, what *happened* to you?" Then she began to cry.

Every time he asked for her she felt slightly giddy. She found herself day-dreaming through the lectures she attended or the odd jobs she was given. She was now free of the Shadows and living in a little cottage on the outskirts of Eidos. Sylvia Plath, who had orbited out of her world almost completely, began to interest her again. She was pleased to see her father and her Aunt Prue when they visited her from their quite different Catholic worlds, but they were only diversions from Kiran. She enjoyed playing the cello as much as ever, but even that was little more than killing time between visits from him. Or visits *to* him. For he made her feel there was nothing he would rather do than spend time with her, and she didn't hesitate to invite herself into his life over at Ganesh and Aaji's.

She was amazed by the change in him and the reversal of their old roles. Whereas before it had been she who loved and desired with the greater force, now it seemed to be he. This new arrangement made her glow. No one ever before had found her company more desirable than she found his. She began to get used to the idea, the feeling, that she was valuable and lovable. She even began to test Kiran's love. To what lengths would he not go to please her? Would he create for her a new sofa if she wanted him to? He wasn't very good at such things, but he did his best. Would he dematerialize it if she didn't like it? That too.

"No, darling, I was just teasing you," she would say.

He lived, it seemed, to please her. When she grew testy, as she often did – for she found Eidos strangely boring and unchallenging in spite of all its beauty – she would vent her anger. But he would always soothe her, absorb her petulance, return it repackaged as cheer.

Sometimes he was stern and played the part of the wise father. She didn't know whether to be impressed or amused. In any case the advice always seemed alien, way beyond her reach. He didn't love her any less because she failed to take it.

She was like a seal basking for a while on a warm rock after swimming across a vast, cold, monster-infested ocean.

There came a time when their relationship changed. He became to her what a faithful, good husband on earth becomes to his wife of long-standing. So consistent, so generous was his love that she began to cash in on the interest that it earned. The world of greater Eidos, its thrilling ideas, its great movements, its endless learning opportunities, its unspeakable beauties, the knowing, "gazing" Light that raised every emotion and thought to an intensity and clarity unknown in lower worlds – all this she finally began to notice. Kiran gradually became more like a beloved companion than a lover in the earth sense: He was her true friend, the first she remembered ever having. But he was also a little like a counselor: She began to trust his grasp of things, to rely on him, to seek his advice whereas before she would merely tolerate it.

She had never gone to school to learn about the "process of becoming," or rebirth. When she first heard a rumor of it, she was shocked, could scarcely believe it was possible, and acted as if it in fact were not. But gradually, in spite of herself, she began to wonder. She had never been able to fit Eidos into her primitive earth concept of the Catholic afterlife with its heaven, hell, and purgatory. In Eidos there was no enthroned Heavenly Father to adore, and surely purgatory wouldn't have contained a Kiran who loved her. And if the Shadowland was just another term for hell, she had exited it! But the idea that Eidos was a place between earth lives frightened her. The very word for reincarnation in the Eidosian language made her nervous, for it no longer carried overtones of pagan delusion, but of truth.

As she opened herself to the greater world of ideas and creativity that Eidos provided, she began to wonder consciously about this forbidden subject. One day she asked Kiran outright about it.

"It's an option. Apparently most of us take it, especially if we've died young," he said.

"So it really *happens?*"

"No doubt about it. No one could have been more surprised than I."

Secretly, so secretly she scarcely knew it herself, she had been hatching a plan around this notion. "Then I don't have to stay here. I can leave any time?"

"You can, but the timing is important. Don't be in a hurry; that could lead to disaster. If you're patient, you'll find an appropriate vehicle."

"Vehicle? Do you mean a mother?"

"I mean a body. But, yeah, parents too. The right family. The right body. But if you hurry, you could end up anywhere. It's mysterious, beyond anyone's understanding here, infinitely complex. But the process is controllable. And there is competition for positions."

"Positions?"

"Souls wanting the same body."

"Hmm. Like trying to catch a cab on New Year's Eve in New York," she joked.

"Or back home on Ganesh Chaturthi," Kiran laughed. "Aaji compares it to awarding a settlement in court. It's all very fair. There are no bribes."

"Isn't that ridiculous?" said Shalini. "I was born into a religion that knows nothing of this, and yet everybody born into it has just gone through it!"

"Ganesh says it's a blessing we forget. Since seeing you last I got up the courage to look into my previous life – not the last one but the one before – and do you know what I found? I was an irascible brahmin priest and a rather cold-hearted husband. When I died, my wife hated me. Thank God for forgetting!"

"Good God, Kiran, what a terrible man you were! To think I loved such a man!"

Then he grew very serious and said, "I don't think you did."

She felt surprise, but only for an instant as the remark struck her with revelatory force. Of course she hadn't loved him. She had merely wanted to possess him, to devour him, to be loved *by* him. She took his hand and looked searchingly into a face that on earth kindled in her a grand passion but now kindled something less volatile, cooler, deeper, purer. "You are right, O wise one," she said, not able to resist a tease even on the heels of a revelation. "You are right, Kiran. What I feel now might pass for love, but what I felt then was merely passion."

"Shalini, you delight me," he said, said for the hundredth time since her "rescue." "I could never have understood this truth before

Judgment. Your understanding is more typical of someone who has been through it."

She squeezed his hand tightly and said with overwhelming conviction, "Kiran, I *have* been through it! I just don't want to go through it again!" Then for some inexplicable reason she began to cry.

As they strolled along the shore beside the river, they were again on the subject of rebirth.

"If you've had a previous life as a nasty brahmin priest, then I must have had one too," she said.

"I presume so," said Kiran.

"Well how do I find out about it?" She felt nervous and excited.

"Are you sure you want to?"

"You already know about it, don't you! I was your wife, wasn't I? Your long-suffering wife. No, I was your mistress! Which was I, my Lord?" she teased.

"I didn't have a mistress. Actually I'm sure we didn't know each other. We lived on different continents."

"Too bad. All those yarns about people coming back together again and again is just romantic nonsense, right?"

"You're asking the wrong person, Shalini. But I'm afraid so."

"Seriously, how do I find out about my previous life?"

"Don't get sidetracked like I did. Go through Judgment first."

"Why does it always come back to that? Haven't I suffered enough?"

"You've suffered in the wrong way. You've scourged yourself without pity, but that's not how Judgment works."

"Well, how does it work?"

"I'll tell you this much. It's completely beyond description. It's humiliating, intolerable, unendurable – yet it's the best thing that can happen to you. It's not something to look forward to, but the aftermath is blessed and good beyond imagining. Do you remember how you refused to believe I was really me until I passed that quiz you created? *That's* what Judgment does to you. It changes you, softens you. I hope you'll agree it's for the better?"

"I don't know," she teased. Then she grew sober again. "Kiran, I'm not ready for Judgment. I've been thinking about this. I'd rather go back to earth." She paused. Now was the time to spring it. "But only if you'll come back with me."

"What do you mean?"

"Isn't that possible?"

"I don't know." Kiran frowned. "Things like that might occur, of course. I can ask Ganesh."

"Then you would like to come back with me?"

"I don't – I don't know, Shalini. I often long for earth, I admit. I'm a commoner here. And the Light still oppresses me sometimes. I don't know why. Aaji and Ganesh bathe in it as if it were spring water and call it God."

"God?"

"It's as much as we're allowed to see of God on this low plane, they say."

"God?!"

"That's what they say."

"Well, why doesn't he show his holy face?!" For some reason she felt angry at God, at Kiran, at everything she took to be masculine. Kiran's mind remained a waiting, noncommittal blank. She took it as an insult.

"So you won't come with me." Suddenly she felt incensed. "Then go along with all the others! Go, go, go along with all the hypocrites! Go on! You and your Light make me sick! God makes me sick! GO ON!"

She found herself alone in front of Aaji's house.

Chapter 19

FORGOTTEN were all the joys and torments she had known since her departure from earth long ago. Forgotten were the Light-filled people whose mere presence made her despise what she was and, like gravity collapsing an exhausted star, crushed her into a dense nothingness. Forgotten was the orgy of self-torture in atonement for her suicide, the bones of small animals arranged and stacked by species and type her only companions, and the gouging of her body by those same bones her one mad pastime. Forgotten were the lectures and therapy sessions and the odd jobs assigned her and – after so much vacillation – the agonizing ordeal of Judgment she had finally tackled head on. Forgotten was all that groundwork before she conceived of the thing she had to do.

Forgotten was the memory of her last rendezvous with the oven, and how she entered again into her dying and felt the consuming self-pity over not being good enough for Kiran and the loathing for that shiny-eyed vixen Lisa. Forgotten was the turning point when she flung out a final S.O.S., an earnest, humble prayer for help to a God or to anyone else who might hear, and the miracle that, she knew not how or why, had begun from that point: the love that Kiran showed her as he gradually won back her trust, the feeling in her bones that in spite of everything she had done, all the waste and destruction she had wrought, she was a marvelous creation nonetheless.

Forgotten was the final meeting with Kiran when she played for him in the healing ambience of Eidos the cello sonata that she – she, not Bach or Beethoven or one of Eidos' famous composers – had written in his honor after he gave her the promise she had sought since their reconciliation. Forgotten was the way they embraced on the terrace and looked out over the river at the forested far shore; the water lapping against the beach; the fresh air and the cool breeze fanning their dimly glowing bodies. Forgotten was the time they confided how, for reasons they could not help feeling ashamed of, they missed earth, and talked of the thing she knew she had to do.

Forgotten was that last emotion that beamed out of Kiran's body, that rich and ambiguous feeling of something infinitely wonderful and tragic at the same time, and the way he said mysteriously, disconnectedly, as if out of a trance, as if he were some kind of wise man, "Nothing burns in hell except self-will," and the way they had gradually, almost imperceptibly merged in ecstatic union, their bodies occupying a single form generally ovoid and glowing with iridescent light and their minds converging on and agreeing on and celebrating the thing she knew she had to do.

Forgotten were all the explanations about how the thing was accomplished, about priorities among souls seeking rebirth in a particular "vehicle," about the fertilized egg cell acting as a "receiver," about the process of "karmic resonance" which attracted the single most appropriate sperm cell to the egg, and all the other bewildering fuss of preparation. And the waiting, the interminable waiting, the feeling that, as in a Kafka novel, there would never be an end to the process, even the great event itself, the moment of conception when, after almost giving up, she finally broke through into matter in a numbing explosion, that too she had forgotten.

Forgotten was the jumping back and forth of her consciousness between brilliant Eidos and the oceanic sleep of the dark womb with its dreamy sensations as she gradually became acclimated to physical life following conception. Eventually all the memories of Eidos, of her past life on earth, of shadowy Hades and the vivid but unreal earth dreams in between, even of Kiran's promise – the entire sequence with its temporal, hierarchically arranged divisions – turned into a churning phantasmagoria of chaotic, uninterpreted memory. The individual memories did not disappear; rather, as she surrendered to the drowsy pull of earth and gave up her hold on Eidos, they dug their way into the subterranean hives of her deep unconscious, leaving in their wake the crisscrossing snail trails of a place and a time ever more remote. By the time of the birth shock, they had all but faded away from consciousness. The unique soul, the sliver of divinity that had played at being Shalini for one lifetime and that bore her stamp in the form of unconscious drives and talents was as intact as ever; but at the level of conscious memory Shalini had all but ceased to be. Only in the deep corners of the unconscious did she exist.

She came into the world in a blast of cold air and diffuse light. The shock catapulted her out of her tiny body, and the light of Eidos, of the world of spirit, flickered for a moment in her dazed consciousness. Then she settled comfortably again into her new body made of clay. She dozed, sucking at something soft and tasty and very very ancient. She had no idea what it was. She did not remember what family she had been born into or that she had accomplished at last the thing she had to do. She did not hear the elderly woman with the platinum blonde hair whose name was Lisa say, "Isn't she adorable?" or the younger woman on the bed, the woman with the soft tasty thing whose name was Sonya, say, "You'd better like her, Mom; you two will be spending a lot of time together."

Chapter 20

CRADLED in a body the size of a mustard seed inside the womb he chose, Kiran dreamed and waited. In his dreams he traveled in his earth body as the Kiran Kulkarni of old. When he woke, or rather half woke, he felt as if he lay in a warm bog of rich humus. The dense air around him glowed in friendly hues of deep green, blue, and velvet against a background of black. It wafted along like dark receptive cirrus, hugging the ground like fog. He felt like a small child resting in his mother's arms in a rough cabin back in the woods, with crickets and frogs providing a reassuring hum, a lullaby of undifferentiated, drowsy sound that made distinct concepts and memories melt into each other and cancel each other out in a vigil of forgetting.

Sometimes he woke up completely, and then he found himself out of the womb and back in his house on Eidos, now empty of Aaji and Ganesh. At these times – he thought of them as furloughs – he moved freely around Eidos as if he were a regular citizen. But he wasn't. An invisible umbilical cord, a bridge stretching from one dimension to another, linked him to his tiny new body of flesh. This body was uniquely his, as much as the snail's shell which it crawls away from for a little while is the snail's. He knew he could not stay away long, or the body would die. And that, for a soul wanting flesh, would be a great setback.

He had never felt completely comfortable in the Light of Eidos anyway. He couldn't pretend he was altogether unhappy to leave it. He was immature; all his teachers told him so in their kindly way. The Light felt like a perfectly wise father, and Kiran felt like a prodigal son chafing under the father's expectations. Why, after twenty-three years of steady effort and – it seemed at times – progress, did a part of him delight in his escape from the fatherly Light?

He told himself to look ahead, to be glad for the special opportunities that only earth could give, to admit he was better off "repeating the grade." Besides, there were all the closures in his present life that seemed to point to this moment as the right time to make a clean break with Eidos.

Aaji and Ganesh had left him, gone into the Plane of Flame, the next level up where the distinctions of race and religion and class disappeared. They had cast off their beautiful bodies of color and form. Kiran missed them so much that once, out of desperation, he trespassed into their world in an attempt to find them. Temporarily putting aside his comfortable astral form, he wore only a flame-shaped "outline" of emotional thought. The effect of that world with its indescribable brilliance maddened him. His mind's intensity multiplied by a factor of ten, his feelings moved between swoons of despair and ecstatic contemplation, his freedom seemed boundless and terrifying. If Eidos was a comfortable place for the generous-hearted, the Plane of Flame was comfortable for the contemplative. The thoughts and feelings of the souls he met delighted him at first, but their inner life, their bewildering knowledge of spiritual realities far beyond his understanding, and above all their joy and love threw him into confusion. He was not ready for the full blast of diviner worlds. The sunbeam that he was, the Imprisoned Splendor, would be absorbed back into the Sun if he entered them; he would not hold together as an individual. The exultation and love native to them were fit for a Buddha, or even a Ganesh or Aaji. Now he understood why so few on earth came directly to this plane. They were savages in the presence of Christs. He never found Aaji and Ganesh. Sometimes he visited his parents, who by now had died and lived together in one of the Hindu worlds.

It seemed to him that only Nigel greeted him with unconditional love. But Nigel was getting restless, readying himself for the plunge that buried memories in the deep unconscious, looking for a situation of his own. He too would be gone soon. As for old loved ones back on earth, no one remembered him much anymore, and his books were gathering dust on library shelves. He envied those Mexican Catholics who were remembered as ancestors on the Day of the Dead and came down to earth to party unseen with their descendants. If only Ravi or Sonya thought he was reachable! But he had raised them to think such things ridiculous.

Eidos had become a world almost lonely. He was drifting away from its society, turning inward. Over and over he told himself he didn't belong. Wasn't Eidos too spiritual for his coarse, primitive intelligence? He thought more and more of earth, that world of dense sensation where he would feel completely at home because completely cut off from the soul-bullying Love of higher worlds. Not only did he long for it at the level of instinct; in a humble act of what felt like unusual clear-sightedness he concluded that God, whatever God in the end might prove to be, and everyone else would be better served if he dived back into flesh again.

In spite of all these reasons, Kiran resisted. The thought of leaving Eidos by the downward track rather than the upward, of going back to earth and doing again all the things he had already done, of taking the low road, seemed degrading.

Given enough time, couldn't he be happy living in Eidos? Couldn't he even get accustomed eventually to the Plane of Flame? Would it feel so alien the second time? Couldn't he learn to adjust? But every time he was tempted not to go back to the womb, to give up all rights to that tiny fetus and let it "spontaneously abort," as earth put it, he remembered Shalini and the promise he made her.

He always ended by going back.

The time for decision couldn't be put off any longer. Kiran went outside and walked upstream under the arching gulmohar trees with their flame-red blossoms lining the thin beach. The Source, the Great Architect, the Mighty Idea, the Celestial Mother, the Heavenly Father, or whatever else one might call the Light, bathed all Eidos in its changeless, unobtrusive intimacy. Often he took it for granted, forgot it almost entirely. Sometimes it annoyed him, stuck to him with a kind of clamminess, like high humidity. Now he basked in it, perceived it as sharply as if it had been a diamond in front of him rotating under sunlight. He felt its subtle responsiveness, its good intent. He couldn't begin to comprehend its emotional nature, but he felt entirely safe and uniquely valued in its vast, unfathomable good will.

He walked on under the gulmohars and paid attention to the beautiful songs of birds coming from the forest, and for a moment he forgot. But then he remembered for the thousandth time the tiny body of flesh waiting to claim him – claim him completely, swallow him, shut out the light of Eidos for another lifetime. He would have to go back soon or it would die. Very soon. For the thousandth time he tried to talk himself out of it. He made the promise to Shalini five years ago when conditions were different, didn't he? Wouldn't Shalini release him from it today if she could? Wouldn't she even command him to break it – just as he would if their situations were reversed? But how could he know for sure, how could he know? He thought of the warm, dreamy, eclipsed world of flesh. The dense pleasures of food and sex again raised their siren call, and again he felt their attraction. Matter – resistant, hard, painful, death-dealing – seemed almost savory, and he knew he could learn to enjoy the game again. Especially alluring was the thought of sleep, forgetting for a time the burden of being oneself, nightly oblivion in the earth's darkness. Oh to be able to rest and forget! He remembered earth's habits–sex with Lisa, the thrill of publishing, the trouncing of weaker opponents in philosophical debate, the awards and grants, the women who wanted him, Ravi's soccer matches, the stock market, golfing with his few friends – all the things that entertained him and cluttered his days and nights and made him forget who he was and what he had come to earth for in the first place. He remembered all the delights of earth, all the merciful games of forgetting. And he wanted them again.

But then he thought of the Eidosian language, so clear, precise, and expressive. Did he really want to leave that behind? But it wasn't only the language that was different; it was the *isness* of Eidos. Everything here was somehow more real. Earth seemed like the faulty imitation of a masterpiece of astounding artistry, and his mind, so murky and balky back in the physical, here penetrated to the core of things, sucking up their unique truth or beauty with ease. Even though he wasn't anyone special compared to the many better minds of Eidos, he could quickly cut through and solve the most ponderous philosophical puzzles.

Did he really want to go back to that dense, unwieldy condition called earth?

He remembered how he felt when Aaji first led him out of the recovery center into Eidos after being healed of "the philosopher's disease," that earthly habit of doubting everything that the senses didn't know. He realized again that the old concepts and language of earth, the old logic, were inadequate.

How could he stand to give all this up? How could he allow himself to be drugged into forgetting the unity of all existence, that most exquisite and difficult perception that at times he almost had, and that Vedanta had tried to teach him back on earth? How could he bind himself to new parents and new children and suffer losing them all over again? How could he bury his hard-earned wisdom and risk losing all sight of his soul, its deathlessness, its destiny, as he had done before?

But then he thought of Velma Stein, his alcoholic mother-in-law. She could make anyone want to escape Eidos! Deeply earthbound, she swiped away his promptings as if they were annoying insects. She had reached the point of delusion where she denied her own death and, like many of the addicted who die, yoked herself to whatever addict back on earth she could possess. In her case that meant going from one drunk to another, hanging around them, secretly and unseen urging them on, thinking she was doing the drinking instead of them, yet never getting the high they got or satisfying her constant craving. She lived in hell but didn't know it. It was his duty to prompt her, to look after her, to be alert for the moment she might call out of her misery for help, as he had once called out of his and Ganesh had come. The boredom, the vulgarity, the torture of waiting, checking in, nursing along the one person in all creation he most disliked, the unnatural faculty of reminding himself that love did not demand worthiness but was its own reward, its own joy – so far beyond him! Still so far!

And Lisa would be dying soon. He knew he would have to greet her when she came over, reconcile her to him, watch her as she descended into the worlds of dream or worse, help her. Finally there was his son, the college dropout, the underachiever who still dreamed of being a film director and lived alone in a studio apartment under the "L" of the great "Hollywood" sign in southern California. "L" for "loser," Kiran once found himself thinking. Kiran's love for his son had not diminished since his death. His heart still broke for Ravi. Time and again he massed his concentration and projected his prayer to his son back on earth, sometimes visiting him, sitting unfelt and ineffective next to him. But Ravi never seemed to feel him, seemed instead to swat him away like some fluttering gray moth. If only he could reach Ravi before it was too late. If he were Sonya's child, then Ravi would be his uncle. He swore to himself that he would be a loving nephew, that he would be like a son to Ravi. But who could say for sure? How star-crossed the world was. While knowing and loving Ravi from his perch in Eidos, there was no way to reach him with any effect. When there would finally be access after taking the plunge, the knowing would be erased. In the meantime, there were so many things to worry about. So much inner searching to do. And some called Eidos a "paradise."

Earth beckoned.

Sometimes he diverted himself by visiting one of the many Hindu realms. He enjoyed astral Kerala especially, with its golden beaches lapped by the waves of a cerulean sea or its forests of coconut and areca palms standing lean and high along its crystal-clear backwater canals. Many of its inhabitants lived by choice in houses made of thatch, but much more spacious and attractive than their hardscrabble counterparts back on earth. It was a beautiful world straight out of South India. Kiran looked at its people sitting on the sand under the palms where they communicated in groups or meditated singly. He always felt a welcome from them, and the sari-clad women were as open in their friendliness as the men.

India. Wasn't this his true home? He had gone there to visit his mother and do research on the setting for his novel about St. Thomas. A few weeks later he was what earthlings call "dead."

He thought hard about India with its bustling markets, its children prancing about like monkeys or playing games with rolling gourds or climbing tall coconut trees for a cool drink, its diseased bodies, its cheerful poverty and sharp-eyed niggling over what was a fair price for a rich expatriate to pay, its tales of the deaths of loved ones.

Death. He remembered how he felt on the airplane just before his own death. Did he want to go through that again? He remembered again his former scorn for all those who believed in souls, afterlife, etheric bodies, rebirth, all those things so real to him now. He remembered his shock when he saw his smashed, blackened body flung out from its seat in the plane and realized it was dead but he wasn't. Back on earth "realizing you are dead" had been the ultimate oxymoron. But surviving death, that most impossible event, turned out to be the easiest, most natural thing in the world. Eating, playing, winning, thinking, dreaming, desiring, shedding bodies, growing new ones might go on forever. This was permitted. The only thing not permitted was ceasing to be. The only impossible event in the whole universe was extinction. Ha! The joke had been on him!

He came back to the sparkling river in front of Aaji and Ganesh's villa. He lived there alone now except for two former servants from the Bombay days, a couple who had cared for him as a boy. On the other side of the river, other villas peeked out at him from under their great spreading trees, and farther out, much farther, rose a great snow-capped mountain created by a master Japanese architect centuries ago who thought an astral Fuji would add beauty to his sector of Eidos. That beautiful, lofty, distant mountain had come to symbolize God for

Kiran, and it worried him that God was still so inaccessible, so impossibly far away. Keeping away from the bustle of city life in the capital, he devoted most of his time now to working out some kind of relation with this God. Since the ambient, naturally penetrating, but mysterious Light of Eidos was as much of God as any Eidosian was allowed to know, he meditated on it for hours at a time trying to let it penetrate further and further into his soul. Opening himself to that Light was hard work; the effort to understand better the nature of the Light was more work. But if he didn't embed the Light in his deep unconscious, wouldn't he completely forget it once he took on flesh again – just as he had last time? He wanted to be one of Wordsworth's spiritual children "trailing clouds of glory," not one of the forgetters. So on he labored.

In spite of his resolve, he still wasn't completely certain he wanted to carry through with the grand plan. He remembered the invisible cord tying him to the body waiting to receive him. So tiny, only four weeks old; but Sonya didn't even know for sure she was pregnant. If he aborted the pregnancy, she could get pregnant a month later, and the next soul in line would become her child. What would it matter to her whether it was him or someone else? And what would it matter to little Shalini, whose new name was Lisa after her grandmother? What would it matter? He could sever the cord any time. He could do it while sitting in meditation under a sandal tree or gazing across the water at the Fuji from his grassy terrace. He imagined the face of a happy little four-year-old giving him permission to break the promise, then the needy, rejected, blood-smeared face whose transformation became possible only because she learned to trust him. Was he willing to break that trust? He had to decide. He couldn't put it off any longer.

Staring at the mountain, he reminded himself that the Light shining on its snow-covered peak was one with whatever it was that glowed in the depths of his being. Suddenly he felt a love for the mountain; he wanted to roll in its pure white snow and merge his identity with its. The next instant he found himself sitting on its top. Far below in the distance, where he had just come from, he saw a tiny ribbon of blue, his beloved Mandovi River, winding its way into the sea, just as on earth. Now he walked up to the exact apex of the mountain and put his arms around it. He tried to love the mountain, but the vision, the mystical feeling faded away. In its place rose Shalini's two faces, the happy permissive one, the desperate clinging one. He turned over on his back and looked straight up into the living Light suffusing the clear blue sky and asked its advice. But the only response he got was the feeling of its intimate presence and motherly concern. No, there was something else, something strangely new. It was smiling, he was sure it was smiling. Smiling ironically at some inscrutable joke. He was surprised. The Light had never smiled before. Not like this. Not once in all the years.

Then in a flash of insight, as if for a moment he had become a god and understood the whole riddle of existence, past and future merged into a present that was both paradoxical and obvious. Kiran Kulkarni saw himself as he was. He was an immortal being reflecting the very light and substance of his Maker, and a petty, nasty ego as ugly as an oyster fish, both at once. He saw that all his earthly accomplishments had been a sideshow, an irrelevancy, a distraction from what mattered most. He remembered something Jesus had said: "For what is a man profited, if he shall gain the whole world, and lose his own soul?" On earth he had learned to love his children, but only as a reflex of his self-love. Except for them, he hadn't given anyone much worth having, not wisdom to his students or readers, not love to Shalini or Lisa, not close friendship to his colleagues or admirers. He had been masterful at maneuvering people around to do his wishes, but stopping to consider what might be good for *them* was an alien notion. Aside from his charities, his benevolence toward the lower castes, and his legendary study habits chiseled out of dogged ambition, his life on earth had been largely a failure. He had been a cool customer, a rather chilly, detached intellectual who felt affection only for his children. No wonder he couldn't love the Light, the Universal Splendor that pervaded all Eidos. He had never learned to love the Imprisoned Splendor within every self. He was a big brain with a little heart.

Yet at the same time he was this beautiful spirit who tardily learned to love one being, Shalini, with real feeling and for no benefit that would redound to him. The irony of it now made *him* smile, too. The seeming failure was really not so bad, for it added up to something good. Now he realized that it wasn't so much for Shalini that he should honor his promise, but for himself. Isn't that what Aaji and Ganesh had been hinting at all along? That he was a laggard in the art of compassion? That his heart must be allowed to catch up with his head? That the love Shalini had inspired in him must carry over into his next life and encompass not just one being, but many? That his craving to be a "man of destiny" had already been satisfied, with little to show for it, and that a new life of affection and compassion modeled after his own dear Aaji must replace it? That the ambitious, aggressive, impatient, judgmental, controlling side of his being – his overdeveloped masculine side – must help create and blend into a less driven, more caring, more yielding, more tolerant feminine side? Precious and shameful. The man of principle who gave abundantly to the poor out of a sense of duty and because it was "logical"; but also the alpha male who amused himself to his everlasting shame by playing with and dominating women to gratify his sorry ego. Honor and shame. Both at once. He joined the Light in its ironic smile. And to think that he almost cut the cord linking him to earth and another chance to grow his soul.

There was one last temptation. He would be born a pale-faced American, possibly blue-eyed, cut off from any contact with his brahmin past. For an instant he felt a tremendous nostalgia for that past, for his old appearance and personality, as if the great event about to happen was really more a death than the beginning of a new life. But then he imagined a happy little girl waiting for him, beckoning and teasing him, inviting him to come over. Now he knew, with a mighty YES that shook him from top to bottom, that their lives would be entwined as brother and sister. He had the sensation of something zinging, like a tape measure speeding back into its housing. He called out to Ganesh and Aaji a final time, wherever they were, as the warm, wet darkness closed round him and shut out the smiling God. A gross sensation, sticky and drowsy, enveloped him as he settled into Sonya's womb.

But there was a final irony that escaped Kiran Kulkarni as he lay insensate in the darkness. Never, not once before that final departure into flesh did it occur to him that the Universe – or God, or his karma, or whatever it was that ultimately controlled events – would disregard the pact he and Shalini had made. How could he have known in advance? How could even Aaji and Ganesh have known? How could the Solomons have known? All they could do was assign bodies to souls. What exactly would happen once the soul took up residence in that most precious vehicle, the fetus, was unknowable. No one in Eidos, not even scientists who had mapped out the human genome back on earth, could predict or control the progress of that one sperm as it swam toward its target and beat out all the other three hundred million in the act of fertilization. So sure was Kiran that he would enter flesh as a male that he hadn't even bothered to investigate during his furloughs from the womb what had happened at that fateful moment.

It was just as well. If he had known he would be entering flesh as Shalini's baby *sister*, not brother, would he have carried through with the altered plan? Perhaps not. But why didn't he at least consider the possibility? He knew his personality was dominated by aggressive masculine urges and that these needed softening. What better way for this to be accomplished than by his coming back as a female?

So there he is, headed "back to the classroom." Back to be the baby sister of a five-year-old girl he once knew as an old lover named Shalini. Back as a female. If he knew what had happened to him, would he feel misunderstood, misjudged, even tricked by the Universe? Or would he see the justice and wisdom of its decree? Would he even have embraced his karma as he cut the tie binding him to his old personality? We cannot know. All we can say with confidence is that in the last seconds before his final descent, he felt a sudden eagerness to take his new post in the infinite imagination of God, whatever that might be. He felt like a man sentenced to a happy death.

Afterword

THE general outline of the world you've just left was not of my
own inventing. If it seemed very real to you, as it always has to
me, that's because the spirits who describe it are describing it
firsthand. This is their world, and the pictures they paint of it come
from a brush as reliable as the one we use to paint our earth. Some of
the particulars—for example, the inset 60th floor of the Hall of Re-
cords--are fanciful, but not the buildings themselves. Cities like Vimala
abound in spirit accounts.

If you are interested in learning more about the nature of the afterworld—the world I believe we'll all enter in a few short years--here are
some of the sources I found most helpful. Some were written by spirits
through mediums, others by scholars who have made a study of these
accounts. Of special note is Richard Matheson's celebrated novel (and
film) *What Dreams May Come*, starring Robin Williams. It is the only
novel on the list, and it is the only book I think of as falling in the same
genre as mine. I recommend it highly.

Bibliography

Barker, Elsa (1995). *Letters from the Afterlife.* Hillsboro, Oregon: Beyond Words.

Borgia, Anthony (no date). *Life in the World Unseen.* San Francisco: H. G. White.

Chism, Stephen (2005). *The Afterlife of Leslie Stringfellow.* Fayetteville, Arkansas: Fullcourte Press.

Crookall, R. (1961). *The Supreme Adventure.* Cambridge, England: James Clarke.

Cummins, G. (1965). *Swan on a Black Sea.* London: Routledge and Kegan Paul.

Cummins, Geraldine (1955). *The Road to Immortality.* London: Aquarian Press.

Doyle, A. C. (1975). *The History of Spiritualism,* Vol. I. New York: Arno Press.

Fontana, D. (2005). *Is There an Afterlife?* Ropley, Hants, UK: O-Books.

Fontana, D. (2009). *Life Beyond Death: What Should We Expect?* London: Watkins.

Greaves, Helen (1977). *Testimony of Light.* Saffron Walden, England: C. W. Daniel.

Hare, R. (1855). *Experimental Investigation of the Spirit Manifestations: Demonstrating the Existence of Spirits and Their Communion with Mortals.* New York: Partridge & Brittan.

Heath, R. H. and Klimo, J. (2006). *Suicide: What Really Happens in the Afterlife.* Berkeley: North Atlantic Books.

Heath, R. H. and Klimo, J. (2010). *Handbook to the Afterlife.* Berkeley: North Atlantic Books.

Johnson, R. (1971). *The Imprisoned Splendour.* Wheaton, Illinois: Theosophical Publishing.

Kardec, A. (2003). *The Spirits' Book.* Philadelphia: Allan Kardec Educational Society.

Klimo, J. (1998). *Channeling: Investigations on Receiving Information from Paranormal Sources.* Berkeley: North Atlantic Books.

Lodge, O. (1915). *Raymond or Life and Death.* New York: George H. Doran.

Lorimer, D. (1989). *Survival: Body, Mind and Death in the Light of Psychic Experience.* New York: Penguin Books.

Matheson, R. (2004). *What Dreams May Come: A Novel.* New York: Tor Books.

Moses, W. Stainton (1976). *Spirit Teachings.* New York: Arno Press.

Myers, F. W. H. (1961). *Human Personality and Its Survival of Bodily Death.* New Hyde Park, NY: University Books.

Roberts, J. (1978). *The Afterdeath Journal of an American Philosopher.* Englewood Cliffs, NJ: Prentice-Hall.

Swedenborg, E. (1976). *Heaven and Hell.* New York: Pillar Books.

Taylor, R. Mattson (1980). *Witness from Beyond.* South Portland, Maine: Foreword Press.

Taylor, R. Mattson (1999). *Evidence from Beyond.* Brooklyn, NY: Brett Books.

Tymn, M. (2011). *The Afterlife revealed.* Guildford, UK: White Crow Books

Tymn, M. (2008). *The Articulate Dead.* Lakeville, Minnesota: Galde Press.

Tymn, M. (2007-10). http://metgat.gaia.com/blog.

Tymn, M. (2010-). http://whitecrowbooks.com/michaeltymn.

Whitton, J. and Fisher, F. (1986). *Life Between Life.* New York: Warner Books.

Wickland, C. (1974). *30 Years among the Dead.* Hollywood, CA: Newcastle Publishing.

Wilson, C. (2000). *After Life: Survival of the Soul.* St. Paul, Minnesota: Llewellyn Publications.

Paperbacks also available from White Crow Books

Leo Tolstoy—*My Religion:*
What I Believe
ISBN 978-1-907355-23-3

Leo Tolstoy—*On Life*
ISBN 978-1-907355-91-2

Leo Tolstoy—*Twenty-three Tales*
ISBN 978-1-907355-29-5

Leo Tolstoy—*What is Religion*
and other writings
ISBN 978-1-907355-28-8

Leo Tolstoy—*Work While*
Ye Have the Light
ISBN 978-1-907355-26-4

Leo Tolstoy with Simon Parke—
Conversations with Tolstoy
ISBN 978-1-907355-25-7

Vincent Van Gogh with
Simon Parke—*Conversations*
with Van Gogh
ISBN 978-1-907355-95-0

Howard Williams with an
Introduction by Leo Tolstoy—*The*
Ethics of Diet: An Anthology of
Vegetarian Thought
ISBN 978-1-907355-21-9

Allan Kardec—*The Spirits Book*
ISBN 978-1-907355-98-1

Wolfgang Amadeus Mozart
with Simon Parke—
Conversations with Mozart
ISBN 978-1-907661-38-9

Jesus of Nazareth with
Simon Parke—*Conversations*
with Jesus of Nazareth
ISBN 978-1-907661-41-9

Thomas à Kempis with Simon
Parke—*The Imitation of Christ*
ISBN 978-1-907661-58-7

Emanuel Swedenborg—
Heaven and Hell
ISBN 978-1-907661-55-6

P.D. Ouspensky—*Tertium Organum:*
The Third Canon of Thought
ISBN 978-1-907661-47-1

Dwight Goddard—*A Buddhist Bible*
ISBN 978-1-907661-44-0

Leo Tolstoy—*The Death*
of Ivan Ilyich
ISBN 978-1-907661-10-5

Leo Tolstoy—*Resurrection*
ISBN 978-1-907661-09-9

Michael Tymn—*The Afterlife*
Revealed
ISBN 978-1-970661-90-7

Guy L. Playfair—*If This Be Magic*
ISBN 978-1-907661-84-6

Julian of Norwich with
Simon Parke—*Revelations of*
Divine Love
ISBN 978-1-907661-88-4

Maurice Nicoll—*The New Man*
ISBN 978-1-907661-86-0

Carl Wickland, M.D.—*Thirty Years*
Among the Dead
ISBN 978-1-907661-72-3

Allan Kardec—*The Book on*
Mediums
ISBN 978-1-907661-75-4

John E. Mack—*Passport to the*
Cosmos
ISBN 978-1-907661-81-5

**All titles available as eBooks, and selected titles available in Hardback and
Audiobook formats from www.whitecrowbooks.com**

CPSIA information can be obtained at www.ICGtesting.com
Printed in the USA
LVOW060015031212

309772LV00002B/408/P